# Ad Man
# in the
# Games of 2046

Other Books by Jeffrey Zygmont

FICTION:

I Am Bill Gates' Dog

The Dropout

NON-FICTION:

Microchip
An Idea, Its Genesis and the
Revolution It Created

The VC Way
Investment Secrets from the
Wizards of Venture Capital

www.jeffreyzygmont.com

# Ad Man
# in the
# Games of 2046

## JEFFREY ZYGMONT

**Ad Man in the Games of 2046**

Copyright © 2012 by Jeffrey Zygmont

ISBN: 978-0-9838131-2-5 (Paperback)
ISBN: 978-0-9838131-3-2 (eBook)
LCCN: 2012931451

Publisher's Note: This is a work of fiction.
Names, characters, places and incidents either are the product of the
author's imagination or are used fictitiously, and any resemblance to
actual persons, living or dead, business establishments, products,
events or locales is entirely coincidental.

Free People Publishing
Salem, NH

Text layout and design by
Nancy Grossman
Back Channel Press
www.backchannelpres.com

Cover drawing by Mark Zygmont
Cover design by Jeffrey Zygmont
Printed in the United States of America

To Ray Bradbury and Anthony Burgess,
with a cheerful nod to Ted Geisel.

## ACKNOWLEDGMENTS

Writing is always solitary. But after writing, the business of selling literature once had been a community effort. Large, well populated publishing companies, retailers, and some affiliated agencies joined writers in a campaign to print and then persuade you to buy a book.

Today, in lone-gun self-publishing, even the business of literature is solitary. I am publishing **Ad Man In the Games of 2046** as an independent author. The publishing company responsible for the book, Free People Publishing, is my own, and it's not much more than a name. I do all the work.

The arrangement eliminates the community of professionals who once collaborated to bring out a book. I work with a few for-hire suppliers, but to them I am just an account paying a standardized fee to receive a particular service.

Therefore I am very grateful to have friends who are also capable professionals willing to give me on-call expertise. Even though graphic artist Paul Weston (www.instigatordesign.com) played no direct roll in **Ad Man**, his input about visual design enriches my publishing overall. Similarly, web designer Hyung Park (www.viamodern.com) maintains a compelling web presence for me, not just for this book, but for all of my publishing projects. My brother, Casey Zygmont (www.zigzygmont.com), gives me general assistance in handling photographs and other images.

Nancy and John Grossman of Back Channel Press started as suppliers of layout and typesetting services, but rapidly developed into trusted advisers who help me find good arrangements for words on paper and screen. John died on October 31, 2011, when we were still setting up **Ad Man**. I am glad that Nancy continues their family business with the cheerfulness, generosity and professionalism that she and her husband together made hallmarks of Back Channel (www.backchannelpress.com).

As much as I profit from their professional help, such friends contribute more in the silent encouragement and inspiration their friendship provides. My own family supports my literature the same way, through the impulse it gives to live richly. For me, living richly means translating experience to artful words.

Thus my children—my daughter Greta Zygmont and her husband Scott Wilson, their children Madeleine Zygmont and John Wilson, and my son Erik Zygmont, Stacy Eakes and their little girl Allie—contribute substantially to this and every book. More credit than this book will ever bring belongs to my wife, Donna, a lover who, like John Donne's lover, "makes my circle just, and makes me end where I begun."

## CHAPTER ONE

Of course he had heard all the tales and the rumors and he had even seen some official accounts of the pain and the misery that came from having the sponsor grafts removed. The disfigurement too. But those weren't the dire consequences that troubled him these rare moments when he thought about the possibility that he too might be stripped. It was only a remote possibility anyway. After all, he was Gab Darby, the highest rated, best paid, most storied slugger ever to play the game. His sponsors would want to keep him well covered. They would want to keep him well covered even after he retired. He was sure of it. So what if his performance had dropped off this last year or so. He still had the name. He still had the fame. Now it was just a matter of getting out with his reputation still at its crest.

And that, of course, was what brought to his mind the possibility that he still could be stripped: the question: should he end it this year? Or should he play on another with his faltering legs and with the ache that sometimes spread insidiously across the broad, powerful muscles spanning his back, the muscles he used to accelerate his bat to such dazzling speeds? He wanted to stay. He loved it so much. And even if he dropped off some more, how poorly could he possibly play before a sponsor, any sponsor, even those not already emblazoned on him, would not want to attach its name to the famous Gab Darby? Strip him? It was unthinkable. Yet still, the possibility crept into his head. Because, after all, anyone still active could always be stripped. The contracts said so. And if it should happen to him, he knew, he wouldn't mind the pain and the scaring. Instead he dreaded only the identity he would lose when he wondered how he might feel to be stripped.

*Why worry*, he said to himself at last. After all, here he was in the final game once again. He had led the team here. He had rallied the players twice already in the two back-and-forth, sea-saw battles that had placed them in this winner-take-all, season finale. Win or lose tonight, he could still retire in high honor. Or if he stayed on a year longer the fans would still come out to cheer him. After tonight's finish he would retain his luster for at least one more season.

*Do right*, he said to himself out loud in his closed and private dressing room. He stirred with a flourish, reaching over his back to claw up his jersey and tug it off over his head, exposing his bare torso, which was his game uniform: the hard and capable muscles of his chest, neck, back and arms, pricked through with the dyes that advertised the bright names of his sponsors—Colonel Chicken, Pepsi Coke, Corolla and K-Wall Stores.

"Tommy come soon," Darby mused aloud, putting on his play-day demeanor as he settled his rump and then leaned back deeply into the power-stim seat. His weight energized the contact field. The chair shot tingling, twitching jolts deep into his being, quickening his heart and calling out the blood surge that engorged his rippling, tensed muscles till they stood out in high relief and stark definition. Standing, he looked in the mirror: *Pepsi Coke* in bright red and blue all across his hardened pectorals.

*Any minute now*, he said to himself. Waiting, hardened and tensed, he thoughtlessly rubbed on the oil that added deep luster to the skin advertisements. Carelessly he worked his hands over his chest and around his laddered abdomen. He smeared oil down each broad, bulging arm—*Shop Luxury* labeling the right, *K-Wal Stores* adorning the left. He banded his neck with the ooze and slowly he spread his fingers down over his shoulders. He reached across his back and pushed his hand upward to coat himself fully. At last the chime sounded. His time had arrived. Darby waited inside his dressing room door for the familiar two raps of his agent.

General Tom, super-sports agent, greeted his highest-paid star with his ritual salutation: "are we ready to rumble?"

"Do right," Darby replied, his ritual response.

Together they strode down the wide corridor, past the indifferent security team and through the lit portal, emerging to the program of loud rahs and shouts and applause from the ninety-seven-thousand live fans packed into the dome.

Darby raised his arms over his head, his fists held closed, and broke into a trot toward the home plate. *Heeeere he comes*, roared the speakered announcer. General Tom stayed just one half step behind him, broadly grinning, trotting himself to keep up and nodding his head in rhyming approval with the cadenced applause that escorted the slugger to his first at-bat. The boy from the dugout ran out to hand Gab Darby the heavy blue

3

stick that bore the printing *Pepsi Coke* on its shank, the words scuffed carefully in Darby's trademarked pattern. The fans screamed more loudly on cue as Gab raised the bat aloft in one hand and turned his slow pirouette. Then they hushed just as quickly as finally he stepped into the box, dramatically to begin his first play of the game that either was or was not to be his final game.

And it went very well for the hero. He boomed two powerful hits that between them scored three runs for his team and he scored twice himself when teammates hit him round to home plate. In the field he made two emphatically scooping grabs to force the outs at first base, the position he played now because it required the least running. The catches were by and large routine and other fielders might have made them without such a fuss. But Darby stretched and stunted and finished both with a flourish that ended with his trademark pirouette, which made the fans thunder as the speakered announcer screeched his approval. Darby's team was up nine runs to four by the final, sixth inning. They were poised for their celebration. The season's new champs. Darby's reputation seemed secured. He reflected on that during his final turn in the field. The reflection—his reputation secured—brought back the question: should he play on another year? It was there in his mind when the opponent's dribbling little hit rolled down the first-base line, rolled squarely toward Darby, who was stuck on the retirement quandary when the ball arrived and therefore through some unaccountable trick of his mind he failed to bend quite far enough to stop the leering little sphere. It scampered between his feet and rolled off into the grass behind him. He looked over his shoulder at it, his feet now spread and planted too late in readiness. The ball seemed to smile at him mockingly from its nest in the grass until at last Darby's teammate, the stunned right fielder, ran to it and picked it up and then fumbled to find a place to throw it. Ordinarily he would have thrown it to Darby, the hero, but Darby hadn't yet moved to cover his base.

Re-energized, the opponents went on to win the game, ten runs to nine.

## CHAPTER TWO

President Jeannie Welk-Emerson-Landose listened incredulously to the battle account.

"I don't understand how something like this could happen," she gaped.

"They were really just taken by surprise," replied Adjunct General Nelson Pierce.

"But how? How," stammered President Welk-Emerson-Landose. "How could they be taken by surprise like that? These were supposed to be our best."

"They are our best. Were our best."

"Then how could they all get killed?"

The general shifted uncomfortably in his chair. He wondered if she was expecting him to go through the whole story again.

"It was really just a case of bad command," he ventured. He watched President Welk-Emerson-Landose, looking for some indication of what she expected to hear. Or hear again. He couldn't tell. She wasn't looking at him. Instead, with her head turned to the side she stared at the wall in vexed irritation. He waited. She didn't move.

"No one knew the lieutenant was married to her," the general continued. It irritated him to have to run through the whole story again, but he didn't see what else he could do. "That was a blatant violation of regulations," he said. "That's why they kept it so secret. We would have never let the lieutenant retain his command if we had known that the two of them were married."

"Then you should have a better way of finding those things out."

"I can assure you that in the future ..." The general's voice trailed off, leaving the assurance unuttered, because he knew there was no way the Army could ever keep its people apart.

General Pierce glanced across at First Adviser Mel Santee. Santee had been silent so far through the meeting. When their eyes met the general raised his brow in a sort of shrug, asking Santee with the gesture what the general should do. He really didn't want to run through the whole story again. But Santee returned the general's quiz with a shrug of his own. He didn't know either what the general should do. The two men gazed at each other for a moment, each silently wondering.

"I don't see what difference them being married would make anyways," said President Welk-Emerson-Landose at last.

"Well, it's because he loved her," replied General Pierce.

"Love? That doesn't have anything to do with it."

"But that's why he didn't order the second squad up to join the fight."

The President continued to stare away at the wall, so that

the general couldn't quite see her face. He wondered if she was waiting for more. He looked across at the first adviser again. This time Santee shrugged more plainly and emphatically, to show that he also didn't know what the President expected. Pierce heaved inwardly with irritation. He figured he'd better just run through the whole story again. From the very first shot.

"Nobody thought anything like this could happen," he began. "Especially not from the reports we were furnished by Central Intelligence. According to every indication, we were engaged in a Standard Deterrent Action. So that when the first assault hit Lieutenant Ready's lead squad he did exactly the right thing. He hunkered down and, from what we've been able to determine, he ordered his command to not return fire. I want to be absolutely emphatic on that point: we did not initiate contact and in the early stages of the action we did not return fire. Those people followed standing orders very admirably. In that regard at least, they performed with honor and distinction: they did not engage the enemy.

"But a little while into it, when it became appropriate, they undertook some standard dispersing fire. That should have been enough. According to all the reports you had sent to us from Central Intelligence, given our weapon superiority and all —the superiority we thought we had—that should have been enough. The problem was, more and more non-affiliated operatives kept trickling in. It was kind of like Bunker Hill," said the officer chagrined. "More no-fils kept coming and coming."

The President turned her head to look at him.

"Pardon the historical reference, ma'm," said General Pierce.

When she turned back to the wall he looked across at Santee, who also shrugged at him. The first adviser also didn't seem to understand the historical reference.

"The point is," continued the general, "the point is, they should have cut and run. The no-fils should have. The non-affiliated operatives. That's what your intelligence reports told us to expect. But instead more and more of 'em kept coming. Our lead squad took a few casualties. That's when the lieutenant should have ordered up his second squad. They were right there. They were within sight of the whole action. They were just sitting there watching the whole thing. He knew he wasn't going to be getting any relief because we've been under very strict non-escalation orders. So he knew we weren't going to call in an air strike or artillery support or order out any additional ground units. But he shouldn't have needed them because he had his whole second squad to bring up to help him. That would have been enough if he had acted in time.

"But they were taking casualties by then. And his wife was back there. His secret wife, but his wife nonetheless. From what we've been able to determine, it looks like Lieutenant Ready just panicked at that point."

"That's ridiculous," shot back the President. "How could he just panic? These are supposed to be our best . . . our best . . . you know, our best troops. Or fighters."

"I don't understand it either, ma'm," said the general. "Lieutenant Ready was one of our best junior officers. There's no doubt about it. But the intangible here is the woman. His wife. She and the lieutenant were married. We know that now. And it looks like he simply refused to put her in harms way. For a while he probably thought he was okay. The no-fils were all out in front of him. It was a straightforward frontal assault and I'm sure he thought he could hold them off. In fact, he did hold them off. For a while at least. But like I said, their number kept growing.

"The thing I don't get," pondered the general aloud, "is why he didn't just withdraw. Why he kept his first squad engaged in the first place. In the early stages especially all he had to do was back them out and withdraw. The only thing I can figure is that he was shielding the second squad. Staying engaged so that the second squad could stay out of it altogether, because, like I said, his wife was back there in the second squad. That's the only reason I can see for why he didn't just back out under some covering fire from them. But that's something we'll never know for sure.

"Because, like I explained to you before, finally the non-affiliates wised up and they flanked him from the west. That was his left flank. It all went pretty quickly after that. The lead squad was overrun entirely. The no-fils hit the second squad at the same time. They'd been building up and sneaking around all that time, so that by the time they finally hit the second squad they were well prepared: superior numbers, superior firepower, superior positions. By this time the second squad was without command, because Lieutenant Ready, well, he was killed in a matter of a minute or two with the rest of the guys up front—they weren't interested in taking any prisoners. The no-fils weren't. There was nothing for the second squad to do but pull out. But they were already pretty much overrun themselves. They just turned and ran. That's all they could do. It was a total rout."

"How many," asked the President.

"How many, ma'm?"

"How many got killed in this?"

"Thirty-nine, ma'm."

"And only three got out?"

11

"That's right. We have three survivors. We've debriefed them all. Quite extensively. That's how I know that the account I'm giving you is accurate. As accurate as it can be, that is, because none of our survivors were up with the lead squad."

"And one of 'em's the woman?" asked Welk-Emerson-Landose.

"That's right. I spoke to her quite extensively myself. Over view-phone. Just before coming here. That's when she broke down and told me she and Lieutenant Ready were secretly married. The whole thing made sense after that. We were having a hell of a time figuring out why he'd stayed engaged. Why he'd kept his second squad back in the rear. Why he'd behaved so damn foolishly. Jeopardized his entire command. Lost his entire command. And his life. When she told me that they were married, everything made sense."

President Jeannie Welk-Emerson-Landose, finished with her questions, looked silently off toward the wall again. Adjunct General Pierce wondered once again what she expected him to say. Or do. It was Santee who told him, "I think that's all for now, general. We gotta talk some things over now. You did a great job with this. Thanks."

"You mean I'm dismissed," queried the general.

"Well, yeah. You're dismissed."

But when Pierce rose to leave Santee added, "but, I mean, you can't leave yet. I mean, we need you to wait outside for a while. We might have some other, you know, questions or something."

"More questions?"

"Maybe. You won't mind waiting outside for a while."

"Of course not," said General Pierce, making for the door, making some effort to keep his consternation and annoyance from busting through his expression or showing in his gait. The President and her adviser waited until he was fully outside the office, until the door latch clicked fast behind him, before they stirred, the President moving first, pushing back from the broad conference table where now only she and Santee were seated. She bent and reached under the table to loosen the dense, water-soaked towel that was wrapped around her ankles and calves.

"It's about time he finished," she said. "This was starting to get cold again."

Santee averted his eyes so he wouldn't have to see her legs and feet as she slid them out from under the table, dragging along on the floor the low tub of water in which she held her feet, the towel rising up from the tub and conducting the liquid inadequately around her ankles and calves. The adviser knew that if he glanced just once the image would emblazon in his mind: her stout, swollen ankles, puffy and pocked. Peasant feet was the term a cruel commentator had used to describe them. She had been careful and self-conscious enough even before she had heard it. After the label got out, the President grew furious. From the fury, she launched a bold campaign to slim her lowest parts. She had announced to her adviser that she aimed to publicly wear a dress again, just to demonstrate that her feet did not come from peasant stock. Santee had told her not to bother. He'd told her that she did just fine in pants and that she should just forget about the commentator's remark. Certainly nobody noticed that she never wore dresses, he'd assured her. And nobody thought anything at all about the fact that she never showed her legs during viewed appearances, at speeches and hand-shakings and at the summits and state dinners and such, when the only part the vids ever caught was her upper body anyway. They certainly never focused on her feet or on her ankles. So why should she bother about them, Santee had said.

He certainly did not want to bother about them. In fact, he concealed a squeamish disgust that her preoccupation made only more difficult to control. He didn't want to talk about them. He certainly did not want to look at them. In the meeting room after the general had left he struggled to seem nonchalant as he averted his eyes. The President peeled away the water-sopped towel and lifted her pink, distended feet above the basin, holding them there as the excess water trickled and dripped merrily back into the tub. Santee worried if he could avoid looking much longer. The impulse to glance at her feet was a perversion that pulled his eyes all the harder the harder he resisted.

"What is that stuff, anyway," he asked her, mostly just to divert his own thoughts during the gap of awkward silence that surrounded them while the President preoccupied herself with the water bath.

"It's something called epsom salt," she said. "It's very ancient. I think it comes from a little mine up in the Andes. It's in Peru, I think. Or maybe it's in Bolivia. All it does is take the water out. That's all this is. It's water. I retain water. That's all. Soaking them like this will get all that out of me and then I'll look just fine wearing a dress."

Santee tried to ignore her explanation while simultaneously he tried to appear engaged. He held his head at an angle away from her so his eyes would not betray him and slip toward her feet. At the same time he nodded his head slowly to feign interest. He pursed his lips. He gave other signals of comprehension.

"Did you ring for Peter yet," she asked him, knowing that

he had not.

To summon the servant, Santee stood up and walked to the call button on the tabletop console. Peter appeared almost immediately, pushing through the door that entered from the President's inner chambers, not through the meeting-room door General Pierce had used. As he approached, the servant struggled with the wide tray that held a second low tub of steaming solution, with folds of white, plush towels stacked beside the bath on the tray. He used one towel to carefully dry the pink-glistening feet of President Welk-Emerson-Landose. On his knees, silently, he exchanged the tubs, trading the new for the old, hot water for cold. While he fumbled with the tubs under the table the President swung her legs out toward the adviser, showing her feet.

"I think they look better already," she said. "Don't you?"

He had to look. When he did he couldn't chase out of his thoughts the association he had most feared to make: her feet made him think of inflated rubber surgical gloves, obscenely rotund with the digits splayed out like the teats on a milk-cow's udder. He turned away again after only a rapid glance.

"Yeah," he mouthed. "It looks like maybe those salts will do the trick."

They waited for Peter to finish: to snug a fresh towel around the President's calves and ankles, to guide her legs beneath the table again, placing her feet in the fresh bath to soak before he toted away the tray that held the cooled water, exiting into the private chamber, through the door that stood opposite the door that General Pierce had used, which also latched with assurance after he passed. At that signal President Welk-Emerson-Landose slumped down in her chair to show her exasperation.

"I don't understand how something like this could happen," she pushed out.

"Yeah. This is gonna be a tough one," said Santee. "We only got a day or two. At most. Central Intelligence can keep the press convoys out of there for that long. That's no problem. They already have the battle site secured and nobody's going near it. So we're okay there. But there's got to be a lot of talk going on. All the soldiers and everything. Not to mention the Bortincas themselves. In all the villages and towns and everything. You can bet the Bortincas know all about it by now and they're bragging about it and everything. Word is going to leak out fast and the press will start asking questions. They'll want some answers. They'll want us to give 'em at least a little something. At least a little information. We gotta be ready for 'em."

"But, why would they attack us? I still don't get why they would attack us. I mean, who are these people?"

"Who are they? Well, from what I hear they're farmers."

"Farmers?"

"Well, okay, I guess they're soldiers now. But they used to be farmers. They became soldiers when Bortus started his jobs program over there. Remember Bortus's jobs program? To get all those people away from the rain forests like we wanted him to, he signed them up in his army. Made them soldiers in his army and gave them lots of pay and everything."

"Army? What the hell is he doing with an army?"

"Well, nothing, really."

"How can he even afford one?"

"Well, like I said, it's his jobs program. With the foreign-aid money we sent him to get the farmers away from the rain forest. He's got a huge army now."

"And they're attacking us?"

16

"Well, not really. Not officially, I mean. They're not really Bortus's army anymore. A lot of 'em aren't. They got bored, I hear. This is what I'm getting from our people over there. From Central Intelligence. A lot of 'em got bored because there's really nothing for the army to do. So they just kind of wander away. They're deserters, technically. But now there's these big bands of them just wandering around the countryside. They want to go home to their farms. But now our guys are in the way. You know: guys like this Lieutenant Ready are out on patrol. I guess that's why they're attacking us."

"God damn you," she shot at Santee. "You said this would be easy. You said we'd come out looking great and all we had to do was move some soldiers over there with the press to cover 'em and it would look like we were doing something. That's all we'd have to do, you said. Now I got thirty—no, forty—I got forty dead soldiers on my hands and people are going to start screaming for my head for it."

"Not yet," said Santee nervously, rushing to paste over her anger. "We still got a little bit of time."

"For what? What are we gonna do? What are you gonna do? You gonna bring 'em back to life?"

"There's time for a diversion. We got enough time to work out a diversion that can turn this whole thing around. Maybe we can't bring 'em back to life but we can make 'em, you know, like, martyrs. They got ambushed, after all. I've been thinking about this. I've been thinking about it a lot. Ever since I first got word and since the story first started coming together. They got jumped, right? Out minding their business, doing their duty, and they got jumped. By a band of rebels. There's a revolution going on in Bortinca."

"There is?"

"Well, yeah. I mean, there is now. There's got to be. Those were rebels that attacked us, after all. It wasn't Bortus and his army. Bortus is on our side. It was rebels. Insurgents. Subversives. All we gotta do is identify them. Personalize them. You know: put a face on this whole thing. Give them a leader. With a name. Someone we can go up against. A Sadam or a Slobo or a Bin Laden, someone like that that everyone can hate. As long as there's someone like that, a villain, someone that everyone can focus on, then everyone will be on your side. That always works."

"But there isn't anyone, is there?"

"Well, I don't know. I've been doing some checking: Central Intelligence. There's a mayor. Used to be a mayor. Vestin, he's called. He was really popular, I guess. Man of the people and all that. Then he went in the army with everybody else. Then he deserted with everybody else. He's from Dink, the same town this whole thing happened in."

"You mean . . ."

"I mean we gotta go in there and get Vestin. Go on the offensive. That's important too. It's important that we do something. Right away. This guy is our enemy. He's an enemy of our ally, too. He's an enemy of Bortus. He's leading a rebel force that's threatening Bortus. That's enough right there. But now he goes and attacks an American Deterrent Force. We gotta go in there with everything we got to get this guy. And we gotta tell the people all about him."

"Vestin?"

"Vestin."

"That doesn't sound evil enough to me."

"Well, it's a start," said Santee. "He's gotta have a full name. More than just Vestin. We'll do some research."

"And you think we should go in and get this guy?"

"I don't see what else we can do. First, of course, we need to let the American people know that he's responsible for this whole thing. That he rallied the rebel troops and that he's operating in the area around Dink. Of course, we'll have to give a complete account of the massacre, too. It's better that we come out with it first," said Santee when he saw the President shudder at his suggestion. "The best way to handle this is to come out with the whole story before all the rumors and innuendo start. That way no one can say we're trying to cover up. Besides, it's okay to admit we got ambushed as long as we're doing something about it. Something aggressive. The people love that: swift, aggressive action against our adversaries. No one's gonna blame you. They'll blame this Vestin guy. Hell, they'll rally behind you as long as you go after him."

"And I should do this on the news, I guess. Right?"

"I think you should call a special news conference. I think this is big enough that you should even cut into prime time. Interrupt the programs. Shit, man, American soldiers have been attacked."

"When?"

"We gotta do it tonight, this evening, when everything's still new, before word starts leaking out anyplace else. Besides, the programming is slow tonight. It's a low ratings night. There's not any blockbusters on the vid so no one's gonna mind us cutting in."

"Can we be ready that soon?"

"We can be ready. I took the liberty, I mean, I already got people working on it. We'll need to get a longer name for this Vestin guy. I'll make a note of that. And I'll notify the vid networks too, but they're no problem. The only other thing we'll need is a battle plan. At least a preliminary one. You'll have to tell the people what you're doing to get this guy. What you plan to do to get him. We need Pierce for that."

"Yeah," said President Landose-Welk-Emerson approvingly. "I guess we do." She bent to re-snug the saturated towel, tucking it up around her ankles and calves, patting it with satisfaction when she finished. She settled herself more comfortably in the chair and then turned her head to gaze off toward the far wall.

Santee took the cue. Rising again he went to the tabletop console to call for Pierce. The general appeared at once, barely getting through the door before the latch clicked securely behind him and First Adviser Santee spoke.

"General, we need you to draw up a battle plan."

"A battle plan," wondered the general from his spot on the carpet. He looked at the President, sitting with her back to him and her gaze detached.

Santee said: "we need a plan to mobilize our forces in Bortinca against this insurgency. Especially against their leader, Vestin. We need an all-out effort against the rebel leader Vestin."

"Vestin, Mr. Santee?"

"Vestin."

"But I don't know of anyone in Bortinca named Vestin."

"He may operate under another name," said the first adviser. "We're checking into that. But for right now we need you to get together with your staff and come up with a plan for rooting out him and his followers. We'll need it by five today. No later. And we'll need some maps and charts to go with it."

"But, what followers, Mr. Santee?"

"They're the ones who attacked us yesterday in Dink."

"But . . ."

"We have it on good authority," Santee interrupted. "Central Intelligence. We have it on their authority that a rebel leader code-named Vestin has amassed a sizable insurgency and that he's behind the incident at Dink."

"I haven't seen any evidence of that on the ground."

"We're bringing you in on this now, general. No one's been told about it before now. It's been covert and top secret up until now, until we've been able to confirm it."

"But I haven't seen any evidence of any insurgency in Bortinca," said general Pierce. "They're just a bunch of outlaws. They're not organized. There's certainly no rebel leader behind them. As far as I can see they're just armed and bored. They have nothing to do. No jobs. No work. As far as I can see they attacked us because we're keeping them from going back to their farms. My soldiers aren't very popular down there."

"Exactly," said Santee. "We're coming under attack, and now we have to do something about it. The first thing we have to do is get their leader. With whatever it takes. That's a proven military strategy. To go after the leader."

"But what do you want me to do?"

"We want you to go in and root out this Vestin."

"I'm sure that won't be too difficult. As soon as we find out who he is, and where he is, a single small-assault team should be able to . . ."

"No," interrupted Santee. "Not a small team. You have to go in and root him out. With all his followers. We expect a big battle. You have to mobilize all your troops."

"All the troops? Against who? There's no on over there for all the troops to attack."

"But they're attacking us," said Santee.

"That was one incident. It was a small engagement against a single platoon. And they certainly weren't an organized force. They were rabble, and the only way they were able to defeat Lieutenant Ready's platoon was through Lieutenant Ready's own blunders. We've already been through that. From what we've been able to gather, the people responsible for the attack have fled. They're long gone. They headed deep into the jungle almost immediately after the incident. They know we'll come after them. They know Bortus will come after them for us. He has to. They're hiding out deep in that rain forest where we can barely pick them up with the infra-red. It's dense in there. I can't even get in there with a large force."

"Look," said Santee, "we just lost thirty soldiers. We can't take this lying down. We have to do something, and we have to do it right away."

"It was forty casualties, sir," said General Pierce. "Just under forty of my soldiers killed."

"Forty then," said Santee. "All the more reason to act decisively. The President will be on the vid tonight to announce the massacre and to tell her people exactly what we're doing about it. Prime time, general. When everyone is glued. That's why we need your plan. We need maps and charts that show exactly how we're going to get Vestin. The people are going to be outraged about this. Forty dead soldiers. They'll blame you, general. And they'll blame President Welk-Emerson-Landose —unless we show them that we're doing something decisive to get this rebel leader and all his followers. You gotta go into that rain forest and root them out. You gotta get Vestin."

Pierce looked over at the President, who sat listlessly at the big table still, gazing with detached indifference toward the wall. The general thought sullenly of the rain forest. He had seen so little of it. His station in Bortinca kept him mostly in the city. At least in the city he felt at ease. The cities in Bortinca were the same as any city back home. He couldn't say the same about any place outside the cities. He couldn't feel as comfortable in the towns and villages, with their squat, fetid, meandering excess of homes painted gay, patti colors like the shirts he wore only while on vacation, dripping always it seemed from condensation from the steamy air. In the towns and villages he distrusted the aimless and unoccupied crowds mulling the streets, crowding the doorways and clustering around storefronts, glancing sidelong with resentment whenever he passed. The rude, spontaneous forest seemed even more foreign. He had traveled just once into the imposing green maze. Really just into its outer reach, not very deep inside at all, but still deep enough inside to comprehend the riotous tangle of tiered and stratified vegetable mass. He had gone in on foot, walking with an aide on a narrow, scrabble-paved road that might have gone on forever as it disappeared into the dark maw ahead of him. Stopping, he had listened to the penetrating rumble, to the densely intermixed colloquy of whirs and chirps and clicks and flaps and taps and saws, barely audible but enveloping. He remembered the distinctive call from an animal nearby. A kind of cack and buzz that ran on at a rising pitch, like a song. A bird, probably. Or maybe a cheerful gibbon.

"But I can't get in there," he said to Santee. "Not with any equipment. Not with the big Clintons we would need for firepower and cover. And I can't even attempt any sort of sky assault. Not without an Environmental Impact Statement, and you know how long it takes to get one of those approved. They know all that, too. That's why they're hiding out in there. The only way I could get any substantial force into that jungle would be to knock it down or plow it over. To flatten whole strips of it. To destroy it inch by inch and mile by mile from the sky or with those big tanks or something. But hell," he said, "I can't do that. I mean, that's the rain forest we went over there to protect in the first place."

Santee merely looked at him.

"And even if I knocked down whole swaths of it," complained general Pierce, "they'd still have places to hide. I can't bulldoze it all. The place is endless."

"They've attacked us, Pierce," said Santee. "There's nothing we can do to change that fact. Now we have to defend ourselves. We have to defend our interests."

"But I thought that our interest was the rain forest."

"Not anymore," said First Adviser Santee. "I mean, it's not our only interest."

Pierce looked again at President Landose-Welk-Emerson. He wanted to try an appeal to her, but still she gazed detached and indifferently away from him. When at last the general was dismissed to draw up the battle plan, she turned to Santee.

"I don't know," she said. "I'm worried. I mean, what if this doesn't work? What if this isn't enough?"

"It'll be enough," said the first adviser. "I know it. There might be a lot of questions at first. I mean, it'll take us a few days to really get going. To fire some shots. To get something going to get some news reports coming back. Once that happens there'll be so much news that we'll be in the clear."

"What kind of questions?"

"You know: the usual stuff. Were we unprepared. Why didn't we see it coming. Did we do everything we could to rescue those thirty guys. That'll be one for sure. We hafta make it clear that those guys are victims. They're martyrs. Heroes, too.

The villain here is Vestin. If anyone was unprepared it was Pierce. But Vestin's the one we'll go after first."

"But what if something goes wrong," wondered the President. "I mean, what if in these first few days, I don't know, what if something goes wrong?"

"I don't know," said Santee. "I don't think it will. But if we want we can come up with a little distraction to bide our time just in case."

"Like what?"

"I don't know. Did you see the game last night?"

"The game?"

"The season finale. The Green Woodsmen against Harmony. It was on the vid. Everybody saw it. It was a big surprise. The Green Woodsmen had it all wrapped up. They were all set to be the champs again. Then Gab Darby missed a ball. Of all people. It was a simple little hit that any kid could have grabbed. It rolled right between his legs and then Harmony went on to win the game. They hissed him for, I don't know, it must have been something like five minutes. And then when the finale was over and Harmony was the new champs they hissed him some more. I never saw Darby get off the field so fast after a game."

"What does that have to do with me?"

"I don't know," said Santee. "Nothing, really. Except that everybody's got to be talking about it today. If we need a little diversion, that could be the thing."

"But what can I do about it?"

"I don't know. We don't have to really do anything about it. We just have to kind of keep it going. Keep it alive. For just a few days, at least. Maybe you can say something about it tonight when you're on the vid."

"Like what," she asked, looking at Santee eagerly now,

anticipating the burst of improvisational scheming that seemed always to come to him in their times of deep crisis. Times just like this one, when, without him, she might despair more deeply.

"Well, I don't know," he started. "Look at all those skin ads he has. He has more than anybody else. He's completely covered with the things. Those sponsors can't be too happy about him. What's it say about them, him missing the ball like that? They gotta be thinking about stripping him. I'd strip him if I was them. They gotta be having meetings about it right now."

"But what can I do," the President asked eagerly.

"I don't know. Maybe just say something about it. Keep it stirred up and in the vids."

"But why? I mean, on what grounds?"

"What grounds? Well, he's got all those skin ads. The sponsors. Those are American sponsors. That affects our image. Trade and all that. That has an effect on us in other countries. You can say that it's an issue of national security."

"Will something like that stick?"

"Ned Instead is pretty mad at him. I got a report from the network just this morning. He was all set up in Darby's dressing room. He had a crew ready to roll in there and he had one ready to roll in the team room too. He'd bought the exclusive. Ned did. From either team. Whichever one won. When it looked like it was going to be the Green Woodsmen he got all set up in there so he could get their celebration from the start. But they lost. Darby missed the ball and they lost and then he didn't have time to get over to the Harmony's side to set up in time. I guess they started their celebration before Instead was even there. I guess some other vids got their crews in to roll even though Ned Instead had bought the exclusive. So, yeah, Ned is pretty mad at

Darby. I think that will help us."

"So you're saying that I should say that this affects, like, something about trade and national interests and everything?"

"Yeah," said Santee. "Just to keep everybody stirred up about it. I'll get our vid-apprisers working on it right away. And then we'll see. Maybe that will be all we need to keep the whole thing going. If Ned Instead picks it up, the rest of them will grab it too. Maybe that'll be all we need to keep it going. Just for a few days. Just till we have some good news from Bortinca to show 'em."

## CHAPTER THREE

When the call finally came during the evening after the big game, Gab Darby had just settled eagerly above a steaming box of soup. He was barely just starting his supper. He hadn't even ladled the first spoonful to his mouth. With its perf-top already removed, the box was brimming full and therefore Darby had to lift it gingerly to keep it from spilling when he moved it from the table top and lowered it onto the empty chair next to his, where it wouldn't be visible to the vid screen. The call's persistent toning annoyed him. He couldn't move the box any faster without spilling it. He didn't want to lose a drop. He wanted to eat the soup first anyway, rather than take the call. But the tone chimed the cadence reserved for super-sports agent General Tom. Darby had been waiting all day for Tom to call him. But why, steamed the slugger, why did the agent have to pick the instant he had started his meal?

Darby activated the screen. He strained to appear settled

and composed before General Tom's image flashed onto the big panel on the wall opposite his chair.

"How ye feel tidee?" started Tom.*

"Do fine," said Darby.

"We got lot te talk bewt," said the agent.

"Knows it," answered Darby.

"Ye heard en-thin tidee?" Tom asked him.

"Neh. Heard nuth. Ei talked wid neh-bod," the slugger said.

"I talked to em lot. They all wanner know ef yer gunter gew er ef yer gunter play gin nixt yahr."

Darby only nodded, to signify the question had clicked. He didn't have an answer.

"Ye in yer kitch?" the agent asked him.

"Yee."

"Dey real mad at ye."

"Figured."

"Ye scen de vid?"

"Not scen. Neh. Not scen. Not did. Not all dee. Sleptid."

"Dey all talkin bewt it on de vid. Dey shewin it over gin over gin."

"Figured."

"Good thin Linnip made et big hit fer em," said General Tom. "Now dey playin Linnip as de hero on de vid. Et takes way some de attention."

"Linnip de hero?"

---

* In 2046 in America, the working class speaks in a dialect that sings, slurs and simplifies sounds. The glossary, on page 210, gives the meaning of some common words and phrases of the day.

"Linnip he de hero. Linnip he de slugger too," said Tom. "Linnip now he de big slugger. Even efta ye missed de grounder, even efta ye missed et, ye wouldda bin kay. Ye Greens still wouldda won de game. But Linnip hit de big hit et put em head. Dey shewin it over gin over gin wid yer miss on de vid. Et takes way some de attention."

"Ah," said Darby. "Yee."

"I thin te-mor we hefte say sumtpin," said General Tom.

"Say whud?"

"Like say ef yer a-gunter stay er ef yer gunner gew."

"Ah. Yee." Darby paused before getting out the single most pressing question he wanted to ask his agent: "talked ye wid de sponsors yit tidee?"

"Yee. Course. I talk right way wid em."

"Whud ay sayin?"

"Dey wanner know ef yer gunter gew er ef yer gunter play gin nixt yahr."

Darby nodded again, signifying that he heard.

"Whud ye thin?" General Tom asked him.

"Doan know et jus yit. Neh think en-thin jus yit." He paused and swallowed and brought out his second most pressing question: "whud ye thin?"

"Doan know yet nith," answered General Tom. "Et all up te ye. Ye gosta makes up yer mind ef ye kin play more er ef now et is yer time te gew. Ye gosta decide. Ye know whud I allerways say: I'm here fer ye. Whate'er ye want, I do."

"De sponsors," Darby said vaguely.

"Yee?"

"Ei wanner kep de sponsors."

"Ye wanner keep dem sponsor ads, ye mean?"

"Yee. Wanner kep em. ' En also wanner get moor of em ef

Ei kin get moor. Ei doan mind te gew an Ei doan mind te stay. Doan mind playin' gin nixt yahr. Ei do whiche'er Ei hasta sos te kep de sponsors."

"Course," said Tom.

"Doan wanner be stripped."

"Stripped," the agent exclaimed. "Who said en-thin bout bin stripped?"

"Ne-bod sey en-thin bout et," said Darby. "Ei jus doan wanner et ever."

"Neh me players ev bin stripped. Neh of em. Ye know ets true."

"Knows," Darby concurred. "Ei jus wanner stay sure. Wanner kep on wid de sponsors. Evna efta Ei gew, evna efta Ei stop playin, Ei wanner kep on wid em. Ei wanner still do de commies en still do de vid spots en still say all dem thins dey wanna me te say en ev-thin. Jus wanner stay extera fer sure."

"Then ye can't gew missin de ball like ye did jes yes-day."

"Knows et," said Darby. "Ei knows et. Et why Ei askin ye whud dey thinket en whud Ei should do."

"If ye wanner keep on wid em, now et's sumpin diffrent. I mean, if ye wanner git even more sponsors en keep doin' de spots en all de commies, den dat makes it harder te say ef ye should stay er ef ye should gew."

"Bud Ei de slugger," said Darby.

"Bud dey all pretty mad bout ye missin dat grounder yes-day," said Tom.

"Bud Ei de slugger. If ets no-neh nough, all Ei done did, if ets no-neh nough an jus a grounder kin change et aller, den Ei stay on nixt yahr te shew em. But ifa Ei can gew now en still be de slugger en still do all de vids, den Ei go."

"Neh person ev had more sponsors then ye," said Tom.

"Ei room fer more."

"There always be room."

"Ei wanner em. Ei wanner more. Ei de slugger. Ei wanner te kep on as de slugger."

"Kay," said Tom. "Ets kay wid me.

"Do ye thin Ei can dewt?" asked Darby.

"Ye know whud I allerways tell ye: whud ye wan, I do," answered General Tom, his customary response.

"Sos Ei kin gew on as de slugger?"

"If ets whud ye want."

"Dee thin Ei kin git ev more sponsors?"

"If ye still be de slugger ye kin."

"Whud should Ei do fer it?"

"Doan know yet," said Tom. "Ets sumptin we gotter see. Ye gotter lette me see whud de sponsors dey feel bout whud hapned yes-tiddy. Dey neh sayin nothin real yet. Ets still too soon. Dey gotter see ef de people still be buyin. If de people still be buyin, den ye be okay. En from whud I saw so far, dey stil be buyin. Dey still be buyin good. But I gotter talk te dee sponsors some more morrow morning. Dey still real mad today. I gotter see how dey feel morrow. Maybe morrow dey be sayin sumptin more."

Darby nodded, watching the big screen on the wall with growing satisfaction as the image of his agent waxed on about prospects that grew brighter the longer Tom talked.

"Dey real mad ti-dee fer sure," he went on. "But I knew et would be. Et always takes em little time. Et takes sumptin else te happen fer de peeplo te see on the vid en den dey fergit all bout it. Dats gotter happen. Wait-ill te-mor. When I talk to em to-mor dey won be so mad. I-ill remind em dat ye still de slugger, en den we-ill see how dey feel. I-ill remind em of all ye did. Ye got more sponsors den en-body. Neh-bod else got de

33

Pepsi Coke on de pectos wid Corolla on de whole back. Neh-bod. Nehbody wid de Colonel Chicken ye got on de neck. Ye gottem all. I-ill remind em all of all dat. I-ill remind em of all ye already got."

Unconsciously, with great satisfaction, Darby rubbed his hand around his neck where the Colonel Chicken label showed as a blaze of black in a field of shiny yellow. It was the smallest of his skin advertisements, but its high placement made it always conspicuous. It was the one ad that showed no matter what he wore, because it always peeked above the collar band of all but the most high-collared shirts. Even his Shop Luxury K-Wal Stores could be covered with long sleeves on a shirt, or by a jacket when he went outside in cold weather. But of course he never covered any of the labels when he went out. Some of the players, he knew, sneaked outside at times under clothing so that their ads were hidden. They did it for privacy, they said. But the most Darby ever wore in public anymore was micromesh, so that even with appropriate covering for clubbing or dinner his skin pricks could be read through his clothing. Only in the seclusion of his own private home did he dare to wear clothing that concealed his skin. Like now, while he finished his vid talk with Tom, growing eager once again to spoon into his box of soup. Now his Pepsi Coke pectos were concealed and his K-Wal arms were half covered by a shirt he wore privately because he was sure no one would see. No one except Tom, of course, viewing him through the vid. But Darby knew that Tom didn't mind. The star could sit comfortably with sports agent General Tom even with his body fully clothed.

"We-ill say sumptin later te-mor," Tom voiced on the screen. "Primetime. By den I should know how dey feelin bout it fer sure."

"Kay den," confirmed Darby.

"By den we-ill know effa yer gunter gew er effa yer gunter play on fer nudth yahr. We-ill have sumptin te tell de peeplo by then."

"Bud Tom," ventured Darby, "which de ye thin ill be?"

"Which from playin more er gewin retired?" Tom asked him.

"Yee. Ei just wanner knew. Which ye thin et mee be?"

"Well, which de ye wan et tee be?" the agent asked his client.

"Ei thin Ei thin itsa time dat Ei gew," Darby replied. "Ei play nixt yahr effa Ei hafta. Oney mehr yahr. But ef Ei kin gew en still stay on wid em, still stay on widda de sponsors, den dattsa what-ill Ei do. Den Ei-ill gew retired."

"I allerways say: wud ye wan, I do," grinned Tom, his customary response.

When the call finally finished, Darby lifted the soup box no longer so steamy from the seat beside his. Warm enough, he said to himself. Juices reformed in his mouth as he dipped the first spoonful. With Tom's image gone, Darby's vid screen automatically filled with mass programming from a network. The slugger swallowed his first taste before he spoke the code to switch off the vid, watching a face on the screen disintegrate into small, linked squares that vanished altogether when the panel blinked first to blue and then flickered to white as the big screen dimmed and blended discreetly into the wall. Looked like the President her name I don't know, thought Darby of the lost face before the concern disappeared entirely amid his enjoyment of the unpackaged meal. His mind felt cleansed now by General Tom's confident assurances. It seemed to Gab Darby that he had shook off at last the fear that had unnerved him beginning sometime before the start of the big game yesterday. Finally he had vanquished the unwelcome fear that somehow he might be stripped.

General Tom kept his vid playing after the call had ended and after his screen switched automatically to the mass network view. This was primetime, and Tom expected some net-view program to flash into his home. Therefore he perked up attentively when instead he spied the face of President Jeannie Landose-Welk-Emerson speaking from the screen. The President! He leaned forward in his chair as he thought: this might be just the big event he wanted. This might be the very news-cycle change he expected to deflect attention away from Gab Darby. Tom knew very well how the news cycle seldom ran more than one day or two days or three at the most before all of the news talkers switched to another big story. Still, it had seemed too hopeful to really expect that the switch would come just one day after his client blew the big game. But there she was on his screen, President Landose-Welk, speaking news that, given its break into primetime, had to be big enough to bump Gab Darby from the mouths of the talkers.

But, damn, thought Tom, he had missed it all. The President appeared to be wrapping up. She said something about soldiers and about a big fight now in Bortinca. He had missed it all during the call to Gab Darby, and damn, he thought, he would need right away to order his vid to replay. But the President was finishing still, and he listened with keener attention as she switched her talk to, as he heard her say, "the big game last night."

"First I must congratulate the Harmony for a stunning and well deserved victory," the President began. Super agent General Tom looked her carefully up and down—looked up and down the face and neck that appeared on the screen. He had never examined the President's image so closely before. He noted the blonde tinging of her hair. He noticed how it was cropped somewhat and flipped carefully, stiffly and unmoving, creating a frame all around her face. But her face maintained the same, uniform, uncolored consistency of all the other news faces that flashed regularly onto the vid. Tom shook his head in disappointment: from the image, the agent could gather no clues about the personality of the President.

"Clearly their victory was won fair and square, from their own hard effort, and it was well deserved," she spoke. "So I don't want to take anything away from Harmony when I tell you that we can't put up with players from the other side who deliberately try to lose the big game. We're already hearing from American sponsors overseas that sales might go down. It's all a reaction to the bad behavior of Gab Darby when he tried to lose the big game by missing that ground ball."

General Tom's mouth fell open in surprise, a reaction he almost never showed.

"I was shocked like all of you were when I watched the big game last night," the President continued. "And after the reports I've been hearing today about the possible reaction overseas to some of our strongest American sponsors, I have ordered an immediate investigation by my Legal Team. I'm not saying that there is any wrong doing going on here. I'm not saying that there is any sort of conspiracy going on involving anyone other than Gab Darby. We don't know about that yet. But I am saying that this certainly calls for a full-scale investigation. We cannot risk the interests of strong American sponsors in other countries." She cut off the words by clenching her teeth tightly within her mouth, forcing them into an under bite that she concealed behind her closed lips, holding the pose dramatically, an action calculated to square her jaw sternly and resolutely.

Tom sat so close to the edge of his chair that he had to press his feet flat against the floor to hold himself in place. This was a bolder stroke than he had ever witnessed before. The teeth clenched tightly to square the President's jaw was a very nice touch, he thought. And the gesture was perfectly timed.

"And what about all the American children watching the big game last night," asked President Welk-Emerson-Landose. "That was my first thought when I saw the game last night: what about the future of our children? What kind of example does this set for them? We cannot risk the future of our children." Again she forced the slight under bite, concealed, so that her jaw squared sternly. She tipped up her chin as she held the pose two beats.

"So it is in the name of all America that I launch a full-scale investigation by my President's Legal Team of the big game last night. Very soon, within one or two days, I will tell you all the results. Stay tuned till then. But in the meantime I want to congratulate the Harmony for their stunning success that is not affected by this news I announce today. Good night, everybody, and good luck America."

The screen refreshed immediately with the face of Ned Instead, glowering earnestly as it prepared to issue commentary on the President's comments. General Tom spoke the code to switch off his vid. He sat for a moment in the silence, astonished somewhat by the President's bold stroke. He had expected some news-maker somewhere to soon turn the cycle. After all, it turned at least twice each week. Sometimes it turned even faster. But he had expected the turn to dump Gab Darby out of the news. Instead, Tom's client now stood more squarely inside. The super sports agent marveled a moment longer at the President's bold stroke. Then he spoke on his vid again, ordering it to place calls to raise the sponsor reps, whom, he felt certain, had just seen the President too.

## CHAPTER FOUR

Plans and schedules changed unexpectedly even in the well-financed world of sponsorship sports. Gab Darby knew that. And he knew from his long association with General Tom that even a super sports agent sometimes left a slugger waiting and uninformed. Sometimes an agent left a star wondering about a cancellation or a program change that the player really had a right to know about. That he really had a need to know about. Sometimes confusion just happened. Sometimes even big-money events still turned to muddle behind the scene and behind the screen. Darby understood all that. But he didn't understand why, after trying to raise him for most of the day, why he still hadn't heard a word from General Tom. Just yesterday Tom had said that he planned to put Darby on the vid today. But here it was, primetime already. The work day had passed. And still Darby's vid screen stayed blank. Changes and confusion were inevitable of course. But he could think of no reason why Tom would leave him so long without at least a word. The General must have heard Gab Darby's many page calls. The General always took page calls, no matter where he traveled. Unless something was very wrong with him, thought Darby. But what, he wondered, could possibly be so wrong?

Darby sat in his com den facing the room's vid panel, but even in the wide reclining chair he did not feel comfortable. The slugger tried to raise Tom again, speaking the code to switch on his screen, instructing it to phone up the agent, waiting silently while the screen worked through its search sequence. Waiting. But nothing. Tom remained unfound. But by then Darby scarcely noticed that the call had failed. He felt numbed by it now. He felt befuddled, weary and unnerved. He sat silently beneath the screen, puzzled, and he did not even think to utter the code to switch off his vid, so that when the panel changed automatically to network view, and filled instantly with the grinning beam of General Tom, Gab Darby first thought that his call had connected after all. He thought, here was his agent at last, with the news or explanation that Darby had been wait-ing all day to receive.

"Wud ye bin doan?" Darby said to the screen, surprised by the tone of relief in his voice.

But Tom's image on the wall did not respond. So Darby spoke louder: "Ei ses, wud ye bin doan?"

Rather than answering, General Tom slurred over Darby's words before Darby even brought the whole question out of his mouth. The slugger recognized that Tom wasn't speaking to him at all. He realized that this was not the vid call he had waited all day to receive. General Tom was speaking on the network view. He was speaking to everyone: this was primetime, after all. Darby sat mutely beneath his screen, canting his head upward to watch super sports agent General Tom tell all the world about the new sponsors supporting the slugger Smash Linnip.

" . . . showed it all in the big game . . . ," Darby heard Tom's image speak. Through his surprise and confusion and also through the faint stirrings of a simmering rage, Gab Darby could scarcely make out or follow the words. His head seemed to hum. But when he heard Tom say super slugger, his mind stuck on the phrase. Super slugger? He had never heard that before. Was it new? Was it a mistake? It had to be a mistake. It had to be a slip. It had to be one of Tom's customary exaggerations. No one had ever been called a super slugger before. Surely General Tom had just improvised. The title couldn't be official. It couldn't be sanctioned. Darby watched his screen as the view panned to encompass Smash Linnip, standing gap-lipped beside the agent. Darby heard it again: " . . . super slugger Smash Linnip . . . "

Darby gazed in gape-eyed surprise at his rival, bigger than life on the screen beside Tom, who was bigger than life as well, both of them grinning high upon Darby's wall. Darby stared at Linnip's witless smile and at his blink of incomprehension, features that Darby had always secretly so disliked. He had to shake his eyes away from Linnip's dull face. Only then did his gaze fall upon Linnip's neck, high and broad upon the screen upon the wall. Linnip's neck wore a gaudy ad: *Shop luxury . . . K-Wal Stores.* The ad was new. Darby could see it was new because beneath the lettering he discerned the faint, pin-prick puckering, the subtle rawness and irritation he had experienced himself when each of his skin ads had been freshly inlaid. The brittle inflammation always left him soon, after two days or three. And even while it lasted it was almost unnoticeable. Probably just the stars who had themselves felt the flat burn of the pigmenting laser recognized the scruffed irritation it left on their colleagues. But Darby felt no sympathy as he glowered at the chaffed, swollen color band glistening painfully around Linnip's neck. *Shop luxury . . . K-Wal Stores.* K-Wal belongs to me, Darby thought, and he strained to remember back to the original terms and conditions laid down when he had taken the *shop luxury* insignia into his arms. It was his alone, the contract had said. But of course there came after that assurance all the various clauses, as they called them, which Darby always left to General Tom for haggling. What did the clauses say, he wondered.

Darby clawed up from the wide reclining chair and pounded to his small back den. He strode to the metal drawers in which he stored all of his important pages. Darby could not read the words that were printed on the contracts, but still he wanted to see them. He trusted the pages' heft and their fixed, rigid order more than he trusted the mere spoken versions he might order his vid to recite for him. His vid played too many other words. It spoke too many other voices. On his vid he heard all the network chatter and he spoke to Tom and to the innumerable others who called him up. He heard the daily weather report on the vid and he listened to his practice schedule and other such assignments when they came from the Green Woodsmen. From his vid he heard menus recited when he called out for supper. He heard the nagging drone of all the news talkers. He heard his car drivers call when his rides arrived. He heard his bank announce auto-deposits. He heard enrichment exercises. He heard game results and prattle from all the sports talkers. He heard clothes cleaning pick-ups. He heard dates. He heard the time.

The vid was for everyday clatter. In Darby's mind the

contracts stood apart from all the usual noise. Therefore he wanted to touch them. He wanted to rub each page as gently he turned it. He wanted to fix his eyes upon the running strings of words that skipped downward line upon line until they jammed each sheet with brimming ciphers. When he wanted to hear what the contracts contained, instead of resorting to his vid's spoken recital, he asked Antrina, his housekeeper, to read the pages. Considerately Antrina always ran her finger along the lines when she read, so that Darby could see each physical mark that stood for each rich word she recited.

But Antrina was not at his house this primetime. She slept there only on Wednesday through Saturdays, mostly so she could be at the stove early to make Darby breakfast on his practice days. Darby didn't need the big room back in the corner anymore anyway, now that he lived alone. She kept her things there in bags that stood on the top of her dresser and that outlined the floor along all of the walls except in the spots taken up by her bed and by the dresser and by the one big chair with the light suspended over it where she read late at night. Colored or dull, matte white, labeled or plain, square bottomed or tapered so they tipped where they stood, the bags held random accessories of ordinary living: foods in perf-packs, shoes, carefully folded clothing, elastic bands, books, bunched stockings, mysterious papers, soaps, towels, mugs and cutlery. The dresser and the closet in Antrina's room were empty.

But the housekeeper wasn't around to read the contracts this primetime. She was at her own home, Darby guessed—he didn't really know where she went on the evenings she left his apartment. But even in her absence, he carried the sponsor contracts to the kitchen. He spread them on the table so he could scan over all of them. He could make out the sponsors' names on the tops. They were the same names that adorned his chest and neck and arms and back. He looked at the words K-Wal Stores and Pepsi Coke, Corolla and Colonel Chicken. Randomly he turned some pages to peer inside the documents. He wondered about the clauses. Which words, he wondered, spoke about how K-Wal belonged to him exclusively?

Later, Darby walked back to his com den. He settled back into the wide reclining chair. He peeled off his shirt. He peered all up and down his contoured arms: K-Wal Stores Shop Luxury. He tucked his chin to gaze down at the blue and red Pepsi Coke that glossed across his broad chest. He folded his head into the ample chair back. He dozed.

He woke the next morning to the chime of an incoming vid call. General Tom, Darby thought, because the vid chimed the specific tone that announced the general's calls. But when he spoke on the screen, Darby watched it flick to the image of a man he had not seen before.

"Mr. Darby?" queried the man.

Gab Darby blinked his eyes and forced them to gape open. He had just woken up. He blinked again. He did not recognize the caller.

"Are you Gab Darby?" the man repeated.

Reflexively Darby tipped down his chin to look across his chest and arms. A blanket covered them. He must have tucked it around himself during the night. He could not remember. He fisted the blanket's top edge and tugged it away with a flourish, uncovering his illustrated body.

"Yee," he said. "Darby."

"Good morning, Mr. Darby," began the man. "My name is Jamie Leerach. I'm an esquire with the legal firm called People for Sponsor Accountability. I'm calling you today on behalf of several clients who have hired me jointly to represent them in this matter."

"Clients?" repeated Darby, blinking. The image on the screen, larger than a life-size man, wore clothing cut in the old style: a dully colored suit topped with a necktie. The jacket was gray. Or maybe it was brown. Darby blinked. The man looked old himself. His hair was fully gray. His face was lined, and very serious looking.

"Who ye?," Darby asked him.

"My name is Jamie Leerach. I'm with People for Sponsor Accountability. I'm an esquire."

"How ye vid me?"

"I got your code from Mr. Thomas Viljack."

"Who?"

"Thomas Viljack. From General Tom."

"Oh. Ahhh," breathed Darby. The dimness of slumber was gone by now. He remembered Tom's vid appearance from primetime last night. He remembered Smash Linnip. He remembered the words super slugger.

"Where Tom?" the player asked the esquire.

"I've been released by several sponsors jointly to represent them in this matter, Mr. Darby."

"Where Gen Tom?"

"They've decided that it's time to exercise certain clauses in your sponsorship contracts. That's my specialty, Mr. Darby. I specialize in Sponsorship Termination Clauses."

"Rimnation clauses?"

"That's right, Mr. Darby. It's my job to carry out and oversee, on behalf of my clients, of course, the standard sub-clauses in sponsorship contracts that specify the terms and the manner of dissolution of the association between sponsor and sponsoree. In this case, it's sponsors, because, like I already said, I've been released jointly by a group of sponsors to act in their behalf."

"Tom do dis fer mim," said Darby. "Ei doan do de clauses."

"I've already received the release from Thomas Viljack. From General Tom. Of course, all of the appropriate notices have already been sent to you, Mr. Darby. The release from Mr. Viljack and the release from the sponsors jointly. You'll find them all in your ebbox."

"Sen em te Tom. Tommy do dis fer mim."

"Mr. Viljack doesn't represent you anymore, Mr. Darby. You've been released to me."

"Waffer?" demanded the star.

"For association dissolution. That's my specialty, Mr. Darby. I oversee and direct the entire procedure. And I have to tell you that we prefer to move very swiftly in these matters. It's been our experience that it is in the best interest of all parties, yourself included, that we conclude this matter in the swiftest possible way. The entire procedure, of course, takes four days. But in your case, Mr. Darby, we have reserved five days, because of the extent of removal required."

"Remove?"

"Of course, Mr. Darby. Your skin advertisements are more extensive than others. Therefore we're expecting an additional day will be required to remove them."

Darby tucked his chin to scan his chest. He wagged his head side to side to look at his arms.

"Stripped?" he blurted.

"Of course, Mr. Darby. That's what we've been talking about all this time. I should tell you that we've been talking under vid-record, too, by the way. We'll have certified copies of this entire conversation. I tell you that, but I'm not required to tell you that. Your contracts specify that I'm not required. But I tell you that anyway, Mr. Darby. This is all being permanently recorded."

"Tom sey Ei no-neh be stripped. He sey et jus yes-tiddy."

"You've been released, Mr. Darby."

"Ei doan ev-ne nee knew ye," he said.

"You'll get to know me very soon," said Esquire Leerach. "We'll meet in just a little while. The files have all been properly executed. You have copies in your ebbox. I'd like to get started right away, Mr. Darby, and I wonder what time I can come over this morning to pick you up."

"Ti-dee," Darby gaped.

"I understand your reluctance," said the lawyer. "There have been a lot of stories and rumors and everything. But those are all based on early experiences, Mr. Darby. The technology is now very advanced since then. I give you my personal guarantee. With the new methods we now use the discomfort is very minimal. Very minimal. Those early accounts were exaggerated. I give you my personal guarantee that we'll do everything in our power to make this as comfortable and as painless as possible. Our facility is very clean and modern, Mr. Darby. You may even enjoy your five days with us. In any event, it's necessary."

Darby bent his neck to look down at his skin illustrations.

"I'm prepared to send the car over this morning, Mr. Darby."

"Tom sey Ei nev-ne nee be strippied."

"It's very important that we get started right away."

"Tom sey Ei kep em ev efta Ei play nee mehr."

"The contracts are very specific on this, Mr. Darby. They specify that I have the authority to begin this morning. I want to send a car over right away."

"Ei kep em," said Darby, wagging his head side to side as he peered at the ads striping his body.

"The sooner we get started with this, Mr. Darby . . . "

"Ei noan get started," he said.

"I'm afraid you don't have a choice. The contracts are very specific."

"Ei doan ne care bewt contracts. Doan care whud em sey."

"But you signed the agreements stating . . . "

Darby spoke the code to switch off his vid, watching the image of Esquire Jamie Leerach dissociate into small squares and boxes before the screen flashed to uniform blue and then clicked white, blending to a plain panel in the wall of his home.

The slugger sat in stunned silence. He couldn't decide what to do. He thought he should go look again, and look more carefully this time at the contracts that still had to be spread across his table in the kitchen from last night. Maybe Antrina had arrived, he thought. If Antrina was here she could read them to him. But before he could even stir to rise his screen announced another incoming call. It toned in Tom's signature sequence again. This time Darby asked the vid-screen to identify the caller. It announced: Esquire Jamie Leerach.

"Nee," said Darby. "Ne call. Doanna wan Leeresh. Wan Tom. Wan Genra Tom. Call te mim Genra Tom."

But at the flash Jamie Leerach appeared just the same.

"Ne," shouted Darby. "Wan Tom. Call te mim Genra Tom."

But the esquire spoke over him.

"Mr. Darby, there is no reason to be so unreasonable," he said.

"Nee," shouted Darby to the screen. "Off. Stop. Cancel.

End. Exit. Gee off. Doan wan im. Call ovfer. Doin. Terminate.
Why woanna ye ge off!"

"Mr. Darby," Leerach went on, "I assure you that you have
nothing to fear. The procedure today is virtually painless. It's
been much improved over anything you might have heard
about in the past. And beside that, my clients are prepared to
reward you quite handsomely for your association dissolution.
I'm sure you know that your contracts specify that there are
certain buy-out provisions that must be exercised. In plain
terms, Mr. Darby, you're entitled to some significant payments.
They will be made at the end of the five-day procedure, as
specified. As a result, Mr. Darby, I can personally guarantee that
you will not be hard put for income during your retirement."

"Doanna nee be retired," shot Darby.

"But you don't have any sponsors, Mr. Darby. You can't do
anything without sponsors."

"End," shouted Darby. "Call over. Turn off. Why woanna
ye turn off!"

"Mr. Darby, there's no need to be this unreasonable. If
you'll only ... "

But Darby was up, fleeing from the vid-screen with its
larger-than-life view of Esquire Jamie Leerach. He burst into his
kitchen. Antrina had arrived. She stood at the cooker, watching
Gab Darby the instant he rushed into the room. He lunged for
the contracts. Last night he had left them spread evenly across
the surface of the table. Now the papers stood in one orderly
stack. That had to be was Antrina's work. Darby scattered them
hastily across the tabletop again. He stared down at them. He
didn't know which contract to start with, which he should ask
Antrina to review for him first. In his haste he couldn't even
make out the sponsor names written across their tops, the same

names he bore on his body. Before he could clear his head enough to concentrate, he heard Esquire Leerach speak down to him from the vid in the kitchen wall.

"Mr. Darby," Leerach said, "Mr. Darby, you can look in your contracts if you like. But I assure you that everything I've told you is fully authorized. You'll find it all in those documents if you care to look."

"Wha?" Darby gaped. "Ye? Here?"

"I have your authorized access override codes, Mr. Darby. They give me full access to all of your video viewers. I can control them all from right here. I was going to tell you that, the same way I told you that this entire transaction is being saved in vid-record—in full-duplex record, by the way. But you never gave me the chance. I am not required to tell you any of that, Mr. Darby. But I prefer to be completely open with you about my authority."

"Wha?" shouted Darby. "Codes? Howdie ye get em?"

"I got them from the Commission, of course. That's the only place anybody can get authorized override access codes."

"Jus Tommy ims gosta de codes."

"The Commission has all of the codes under file, Mr. Darby. I executed a court order to obtain them late last night. I received them directly from the Commission. It's all very legal. I didn't need to get them from Mr. Viljack."

"Ei gunter kill im," said Darby.

"Kill who, Mr. Darby?"

"Tom. Ei gunter killte Genra Tom."

"I've already assured you that Mr. Viljack has nothing to do with this. You've been released, Mr. Darby. You're now my responsibility. You remain my responsibility as long as you're undergoing association dissolution. It's all spelled out very clearly, Mr. Darby. I sent you the documents. They're in your ebbox."

Darby sprang toward the vid screen, standing so close he could see the pixel breaks in the image of Esquire Leerach. He shouted: "Stop. Off. Go. Exit. Quit."

"Mr. Darby," the attorney said, "I told you that I have override authority. I can control your entire vid-system from here."

The slugger rushed away, scrambling through the doorway to get back into his media den. But Leerach watched him in that room too. As Darby dashed past the vid screen the attorney said, "Mr. Darby, I have to remind you again that this entire transaction is being saved under vid-record. Full video duplex, Mr. Darby. I am not required to remind you of that. But since you seem to be making threats . . .."

Darby dashed past the vid before Leerach finished. He burst into his bedroom. He heard Leerach speaking still.

". . . Viljack is no longer in any way involved in this, Mr. Darby."

On the big screen on the ceiling above the bed the esquire's face looked flat. His larger-than-life head appeared elongated, distorted by the angle of Darby's view as Darby stood on the floor looking up and across at the talking image poised over the bed.

"Canno see-em me here," announced Darby aloud. He ignored the old man's canted visage. His bedroom screen was set to receive images only. It blanked out the live, return picture that went out with other vid calls. Therefore in the bedroom Darby felt concealed. He sat down on the edge of his mattress, relieved for the private moment in which to recollect himself.

"Mr. Darby," came the voice of Leerach. "Mr. Darby, I

know you're still there. Trust me, Mr. Darby. I've been doing this for a long time. I told you I have override control of your vid-system. Even though I'm not required to tell you that, as stipulated by law, according to the commercial release agreements I have executed, I have told you that fact repeatedly. I tell you so that you realize that you can trust me, Mr. Darby. I've been doing this for a very long time. In my experience, the best approach is to take care of the matter immediately. That's why I have arranged to pick you up this morning, Mr. Darby. You don't have to prepare anything. Everything will be taken care of for you."

Darby sat apprehensively, confused, silent, not moving. He stayed very quiet. But the attorney called down to him still: "Mr. Darby," he said. "I know what you're doing. I can see you there. I told you I have override authority. I control all of the screens in your house. I can set them to receive and to send. I reset this one, Mr. Darby. I can see you right now. There's no reason to ignore me, Mr. Darby. My car should arrive any minute . . . "

His car, thought Darby with sudden surprise. He bent backwards to look up at the ceiling screen. Yes, he saw clearly now the detail he had missed before, recognizing it in the narrow scene that framed the attorney's head as he spoke. Leerach was in the backseat of a car. The car was moving. He is coming right now, thought Darby. He sprang up and dashed out of the bedroom. He crossed the com den, hearing the prate of Leerach still. ". . .no reason why you . . . .." Bursting into the kitchen he saw Antrina again, backed against the cooker, where he had left her a moment earlier. He heard Leerach still, now from the screen in the kitchen. ". . . nothing you can do . . . .." Darby crashed through the thick door that led to his building's back hallway. The cool, sparse lighting surprised him. It seemed almost soothing. With the door slammed tightly behind him Darby paused to listen carefully. He heard no penetrating trace of Leerach's voice. Relieved, he strode swiftly down the long corridor, almost at a run, moving for the stairs that scrambled downward to the building's rear entry. From behind him he heard Antrina call out: "Gabdubby, Gabdubby," she called. "don run way yet."

Darby stopped to look back. The dim light framed her silhouette.

"Where ye goin?" she asked him.

He didn't know where he was going.

"Wait jus a sec," she shouted. A sliver of gaudy light pierced the hallway when she swung open the door and disappeared back into the kitchen. The light flashed abruptly again to announce her return. Darby blinked. Antrina ran toward him.

"Here," she said. "Put this on."

She passed him a white paper sack. It had to be one of the bags that outlined the room where she stayed on Mondays through Thursdays. Reflexively Darby glanced upward at the security camera on the wall above them.

"Doan worry bout that," Antrina told him. "The eyes doan work in here. They stopped workin a long time ago and neh-bod's been round to fix em. Neh-bod sees what goes on back here en-more."

Darby reached inside the white bag. He pulled out a shirt. It was large. It was sewn from thick fabric, with long sleeves and a high, concealing neck.

"Whas?" he asked Antrina.

"Put it on," she told him.

"Whas?"

"I had it in my room. I was keeping it for you. For just in

55

case. For just in case something like this happened. Put it on."

"Ye buy?" he asked her.

"I made it," she answered. "Put it on."

Darby tugged the shirt down over his head and pushed his arms into the sleeves that seemed endlessly long to him. He had to push up the cuffs around his wrists and as the fabric fell down his back and over his chest he noticed its substantial heft. The shirt's bulk felt almost uncomfortable. It felt confining compared to the translucent microweave he customarily wore—when he wore any kind of a covering over the ads. Often, when he just ran out for a jaunt, he wore no shirt at all.

But Darby did not pause to reflect or deliberate. He hesitated only a moment while Antrina stepped back to apprise him. She stepped forward again, reaching up to the slugger's wide neck to test the shirt's collar. She pulled it and watched it snap back into place, satisfying herself that the collar would stay high on his neck. When she stepped back a second time she nodded. Thus released, Darby spun around right away, and continued his flight toward the stairs that would lead him downward to the building's back exit.

## CHAPTER FIVE

D arby felt shamefully conspicuous as he stood outside the tall fence with his chest and neck and arms fully concealed beneath the long shirt. He couldn't understand why he had even come here, except for the fact that he frequently came here and therefore, with nowhere else to flee, his legs had paced out the route automatically. At least no one was outside yet, he thought with a little relief. But he knew that very soon the doors to the building inside the large yard would fling open and the children would gush out chaotically. Ordinarily he felt impatient until they first appeared. Ordinarily he felt excited as he watched the kids burst out of the building and spill frantically toward gleeful, unscripted play. Ordinarily he flashed with delight the first instant he spotted his son among the spinning mad dervishes. But today, concealed inside Antrina's big shirt, Darby preferred the barren emptiness of the yard before the children's release for recess.

In the stillness he gazed slowly to his left and to his right all along the distant-running fence that bounded the school lot. He tilted back his head to look up at the coiled razor wire that furled the full length of the high enclosure. Win, his son, had boarded here for nearly two years, beginning with Darby's bust up with Doreen. Terms of the divorce had placed the young boy in the government school. Darby wasn't allowed inside the place. He had never even stepped within the fenced yard. He tilted back his head again, gazing up at the coiled razor wire atop the chainlink. He could breech it, he knew, but the care he took with the wire would cost him a precious minute or two, and he would still most likely cut up his hands in the effort.

Distantly the tone sounded, announcing the children's release. They came as they always came, tumbling through the twin doors in a waggling, mass tangle of small limbs and trunks. The children stayed back by the building, hurling together in a liquid mob that shifted, massed, pulsed, spun, wound, bundled, dispersed and regathered spontaneously as each child within it separately reached, twisted, whirled, hopped, dodged, ducked and ran. Three somber play-aides circled silently at the edges of the kinetic mass, their arms crossed at their chests as slowly they paced, keeping the demons in bounds.

Today as he watched them spray into the yard, Darby felt trepidation instead of delight. He scanned the writhing tangle hesitantly, uneager today to pick out his child. He felt almost relieved when he couldn't fix on any of the dodging faces. He looked away from the erratic mob. He peered at the swings, following each seat oscillation by measured oscillation down the straight row of them. Win was not there. He watched children scuff down the slide. Win wasn't there either. Darby gazed back into the exuberant gang on the asphalt. He discovered Win at last because the boy was not moving. His son stood silently apart from the other kids, hiding, it seemed, in the shade of the meager tree that grew near the pad where the play-aides massed the children. He was staring straight back at Darby. Because of the distance, Darby couldn't make out the expression on Win's face. Still, the boy's reluctance and confusion showed clearly enough in his posture. It showed in the very fact that the child hung back, standing alone in the inadequate shadow.

Ordinarily when Darby appeared outside the chainlink, his son shouted gleefully to the few of his chums who were favored that day, to Lin or Tip or Gap or Yank, inviting them along as the boy raced to greet his father. Ordinarily Win stuck his small hand through the fence to shake with his father the sports star. Their hand clasp was always rapid and quickly released, because the play-aides, who always watched closely, might prohibit even that. Ordinarily, after their customary shake, his son and his son's chosen pals chattered at Darby, asking about his play, about his rank and standing. They were still too young to really follow the sport, but Darby knew that they saw him from time to time on the vid, and he told them always that he was still the top slugger, which had always been true.

But this morning the boy remained motionless. He stared across the school yard and beyond the fence with an expression that Darby strained to make out.

*Blasph es bic shirt*, Darby said to himself. *Win ye doan know es bic shirt.* Shame tugged more acutely at the slugger. He glanced behind himself, looking over his left shoulder and over his right, hoping to spy a place where he might remove the rude garment out of sight of the boy. But the area all around the school yard was leveled and cleared as an enforcement zone. He would have to run too far to find cover. By the time he returned the children might be inside again. The boy stared impassively still from the distant shadow. Darby raised an arm above his head. Tentatively and reluctantly he waved. The boy did not move.

With a sudden flourish Darby grasped his shirt at the shoulders. He snapped it over his back and ducked his head out the bottom as the shirt slid away from him in one whip-like motion. Comfortably exposed, Darby crumpled the rag in one hand and tucked it against a hip. He peered down at his chest. He picked off two specs of fuzz from the fabric that still clung to his skin. Unoiled, the ads shone more dully now. But still they stood out clearly: Pepsi Coke emblazoned across his chest, Shop Luxury running down his left arm and K-Wal Stores running up the right. When Darby looked up again at his son, Win broke into a sprint toward him, his face alight at last. The child nearly reached the fence. He was just paces away from Darby when suddenly he reared to a stop. Win gathered himself uncertainly. He stayed there, staring motionless again, as if some hovering fright waited invisibly in a murk behind his father. Darby inflated his chest and raised his arms just above shoulder level, standing cross-like in the gesture that always drew frenzied cheers at the ball parks. Still the boy stared, impelled from stepping closer by a presence behind his father.

Darby heard Leerach speak passionlessly from just over his shoulder. "This is an enforcement zone," the attorney said. "All enforcement zones are monitored, Mr. Darby. We would have found you anyway. You can be assured of that. But you made it easier for us by coming here. I have full legal authority to conduct a scan search of every monitored zone, Mr. Darby. It's all spelled out and stipulated. Naturally this is one of the first zones we checked. That's how we found you so quickly. You have to come with us now, Mr. Darby."

The slugger turned around to see Jamie Leerach, more diminished in the flesh than he had appeared upon Darby's screen. Two hulking, badged and blue-suited Neighbors leered from the flanks of the frail attorney. Darby felt almost insulted that Leerach had brought only a pair of them. Still, the Neighbors grinned restively, restrained like chained canines. They were brutish. They were trained and conditioned as takers. Darby was large and athletic himself. But his skills were different. As the two Neighbors waited, pent, impatient, standing half a step behind little Leerach, their silver badges glinted with the same, sanctioned assurance that illumined their grins.

"I don't need to remind you that you're prohibited from resisting here, Mr. Darby," spoke Leerach. "You're prohibited from creating any kind of a spectacle."

Standing with his back against the chainlink, Darby glanced left and right, examining the long-running, stark fence.

"You're prohibited from going inside, as well, Mr. Darby. You realize that, I'm sure. That's why the fence is here in the first place. This is an enforcement zone, you know. You can see all the signs right behind you: no drugs, no tobacco, no alcohol, no violence. You know the conditions, Mr. Darby."

Darby stepped off straight ahead, the only direction he could go. He angled a bit to avoid the three men, but he brushed near enough to show that the Neighbors did not intimidate him. The Neighbor he passed the nearest acted first. He stepped snugly behind Darby as he passed, wrapping both his hulking arms around the athlete's chest in an embrace so tight that Darby felt the press of the cop's badge against his back. He smelled the antiseptic cleaning fluids that lingered on the Neighbor's blue polyester. Darby pulled loose the man's grip at the fingertips and ran out of the hold. The second cop arrived, striking Darby mid-section with a flying tackle that threatened to topple the star. But Darby leaned toward the driving shoulder, scooting away his hips simultaneously so that he stayed on his feet. He dodged and twisted and spun around so rapidly that the Neighbor, driven irredeemably forward by the force of his own momentum, belly-flopped onto the pavement as Darby writhed free.

Gab Darby now felt unmistaken exhilaration. He heard Leerach chatter behind him as he dug in his feet to dash away. ". . . type of behavior . . . expressly forbidden . . ." went the esquire. Darby managed just a few steps before the first neighbor was on him again. He gripped Darby in a hug even tighter than the first, pinning Darby's arms along his sides so that this time he couldn't reach up to pry apart the Neighbor's fingers. Darby tried to keep running, lifting his knees for traction to pull away from the stubborn bear. But the officer held him in place and Darby could feel the Neighbor snugging in even closer and planting his feet and lifting, so that Darby began to rise up off of the ground. Instantly Darby threw all of his weight backwards over the cop, bending him downward. Darby sprawled his legs and planted his soles to brace himself upright. ". . . absolutely no reason to violate . . . ," prattered Leerach.

Darby was stuck in a stalemate. He couldn't pull free, but at least the restraining cop couldn't throw him down. ". . . not permitted to resist . . . ," Leerach droned. The second Neighbor, brushed off after his belly dive, circled leeringly, grinning at Darby with his stunner unholstered. He seemed even to pause as he approached the hero face-on, savoring a certain victory. He didn't see the automobile driving up on his flank. The car door was angled open and Darby gaped with incomprehension as the yellow, lumbering vehicle rolled and bumped across the vehicle-free enforcement zone. Even Leerach stopped talking in surprise. By the time the stunning Neighbor turned around the car was too close. He couldn't avoid it. The open door clipped him with a dull, hollow crunk the same instant the taxi veered suddenly away from the wrestlers. The blow had been aimed. It hurled the cop violently to the ground. The car jounced till it stopped. Darby recognized Antrina driving it.

She waved frantically for Darby to come. Energized, he broke the hug of the restraining Neighbor. Darby spun around and clopped the cop hard with his fist. The blow crashed squarely on the Neighbor's cheek. Stiffly the man tumbled to his back and he lay as still as his partner. Even with both cops down, the attorney still moved his jaw: ". . . an enforcement zone, Mr. Darby. The children outside . . .."

Darby dashed for the auto. At the same time, Antrina rushed away from it. Their paths crossed. Leerach shut up again. Darby reached the auto. Antrina stopped one step from the yabbering esquire. She scooped down to grab the shirt that Darby had dropped when the fight had begun. She turned and pushed back for the car, running awkwardly. "Get in," she shouted to Darby, who had waited outside the passenger door. They both swung into their seats. Antrina dropped the taxi's gear lever into drive. The car spun away in a frantic rush toward the streets and legitimate roads outside of the zone.

From inside the auto, Darby peered back. Leerach stood in the same spot still, motionless except for his running jaw. Just beyond him, clamped onto the chainlink, the row of customary metal signs stood like shields in a phalanx: Drug-free School Zone, Tobacco-free School Zone, Alcohol-free School Zone. The last one said, No Violence. Pressed against the fence beneath the signs clamored all of the children. They waved and bounced and cheered frantically as the trio of dour play-aides scuttled among them, trying to shoo the kids back like barnyard poultry. But the tykes merely dodged them. They ducked, hopped and spun as they watched the retreating car with their faces turned up brightly and their mouths yapping open in grins and shouts as they bounced up and down and sprinted around in small dervish-like circles. Through the back window Darby watched the gay mayhem recede further and further as Antrina pushed resolutely toward liberty. He gazed inside the jostling mob to pick out his son. At the same time he wondered if the children were cheering for him.

## CHAPTER SIX

"**P**ut this on right now," said Antrina, returning the shirt to Darby without taking her gaze from the street that loomed like a river ahead of her vehicle. Unhesitantly Darby slipped the baggy black garment over his head and tugged down its hem till the shirt bottom fell securely below his waist. The cloth covered his body completely. Its constraining discomfort returned. Antrina snapped a rapid, sideways glance at Darby to assure herself that the high, rolled collar concealed the lettering pricked into his neck.

"Ye better get in the back seat," she said to him. "This time they kin think I'm a real taxi."

Obediently Darby stooped between the two front buckets. He stepped and stretched and tumbled gracelessly onto the stuffed bench behind his housekeeper. The high floor forced his knees nearly up to his chest. Enclosed in the car, hidden beneath the shirt, he felt cramped and confined. He felt helplessly restrained. He felt immobilized and perilously pent. His lungs still heaved from the dust-up with the Neighbors. He felt that each violent expand of his chest might bust outside the constraining bounds of the automobile, like a bird bursting out of an egg. But this egg was fleet and fast-rolling. It dashed, bowed, swerved and hopped as it pushed among the jostling vehicles that demarced the street that ringed the enforcement zone around Win's school. Antrina nicked furtive glances left and right to measure the bob of the stuttering traffic that suddenly engulfed the car. Most of the vehicles were yellow-sprayed taxis, just like this one, free-rolling and separately contending to rove upon the gagging street. Mostly, like Antrina's, the taxis were Faravans, special livery models made long and boxy, with side doors that slid open on tracks for easy loading. Darby had ridden in hundreds, probably even thousands of Faravans before. None was distinguishable from another. Yet in this one he felt displaced.

"Ye drife?" Darby quizzed his housekeeper, who, sitting just inches ahead of him, piloted the car with more strident confidence than Darby had realized she possessed.

"Yee, yee, course I drive," she answered. "I learnt in Bortinc, like ev-body else that lives there. In Bortinca ye heffte learn, cause ev-bod drives fer em-selves. Neh-bod takes da taxis ev-place dey go, de way ye do et here."

"Ye drife texi too?" Darby asked her, anxious to account for the incongruous cab that had rescued him and that now confined him. His breath still came in gulps, causing him to push out the words.

"No," she answered. "Nee, nee, I'm not a taxi. I drive this fer m'self. That's all. It's only painted up te look lik a taxi, jus lik all the cars we Bortos drive when we live here."

Striving Faravans closed around the car. A bright delivery van bumped alongside. A small, sputtering motor courier raced, spun, dodged, cut, and merged among the moving trucks and cabs, then slanted perilously toward the still, stolid buildings that shaded the liquid pavement.

"My son give it to me," continued Antrina, speaking in distraction, the words detached from the urgent demands of the car. "He used to use it fer hisself, but he got a new one to drive, so he give me this one to drive to my work."

"Work?" wondered Darby. He remained puzzled: did work mean housekeeping for him, or was she also a cabman on the side?

"I drive it to work at your house," she said. "I drive it to your home block. I leave it down underneath with all the other cars that all the other Bortos drive when they come to work at your home block too. Ye seen em all down there, havnet ye?".

Of course he had noticed the rows and clusters of yellow cars always at rest in the dim recesses of his building's drive-through—the underground cavern that was unused except as a pick-up spot where people waited after calling for a car to take them out. But Darby had always just thought they were ordinary taxis, parked out of the way between shifts and such. Why wouldn't he find so many extra cabs off duty, when so many already crammed the roadways? They filled the boiling panoptic around him now, darting like furious fishes.

"Only some uf em are real taxis," Antrina went on in a rush. She stomped and swerved and scooted her car inside a gap that opened precariously next to them. "See," she said, "look at em: Only a driver. Ye doan see any passenger inside em. It's because they aren't real taxis. Those are regular Bortos driving em, jus lik me. I doan pick-up oth people. I only drive meself.

All the Bortono do. Most of us do, enway. It's the way we get round to ev-where: we mek it look lik we-er taxis. If we dint look lik taxis, the Neighbors would stop us all the time, same as they-id stop ye. I cant have a car same as ye cant have a car. But I can have a taxi. Course, it helps that I'm a Borto. When they see I'm a Borto, the Neighbors doan stop me to see if I'm really a taxi. They doan stop me to see if I really have a license. When yer a Borto, no profiling."

A motor courier flashed past Darby's window.

"Least now, wif ye sittin back there, I look lik a real taxi this time," Antrina said with distraction, speaking to the air, the words meant to quiet her own apprehension. "But we heffte git outter here fast. The Neighbors will sure stop us now, after ye had that big fight an after I het one of em wid this car. It's lucky the school is so close to the end uf yer urb. We-ill be outter here fast. Once we get on the connector I think we-ill be okay. The Neighbors doan go out on the connectors with their little electrics. Ye need a fuel car out on the connectors. Their little electrics doan go too far away from their Neighborhood Homes."

Another flashing courier loomed smack into Darby's view. It dashed into the gap that opened suddenly when twin, flanking Faravans parted, and for an instant it cannonballed heedlessly toward Darby's side. It veered away as rapidly, turning this time downroad, away from the flow of traffic that had paced Antrina's retreat.

"Least they woan find me out from any of their eyes," she announced to herself. "I doan thin they have any vids to show en-bod what I did to em. I thin they probably turned the eyes off before I came. They probably turned em off before they first went up to git ye. The Neighbors always turn em off when they plannin to do somethin lik that. They doan wan any proof. They doan wan any evidence. So they turn the eyes off and then they say it was from static or interference or they just were on the blink that day. But ev-body knows it's because the Neighbors always turn the eyes off whenever they're up te somethin. Then they can say what they wan bout what happened. So I bet there's no vids they can look at now to finger out who I am. They'll make some guesses, but they won't have a vid that-ill tell em fer sure."

She leaned forward in her seat, anticipatory.

"If we kin jus git outter this urb," she urged. "If we can jus git outter this urb we-ill be okay. The Neighbors woan go outter here in their little electrics."

But Antrina and Darby were already pressing out of the dense settlement, their progress marked by the sudden veer-off of taxis, as the herded Faravans that pressed close at their sides scattered nervously at angles. Antrina pointed hers head-up, aiming defiantly at the yawning gap of roadway that opened where the building fronts parted. Her Faravan gained speed as the others diminished. The buildings dropped off entirely. The concrete strip widened. A large truck merged beside them as it rumbled out of a boundary terminal where other trucks swarmed as in a hive outside the bustle of the urb. The truck was larger by far than the bright, busy delivery vans that wheeled the streets around Darby's home block. As it raced outside the window that pressed nearly against his nose, Darby shrank back from its immensity. He had never before experienced one roar so close. Darby had never before ridden inside a car traveling on what Antrina called the connector. He had viewed connectors only distantly, from overhead when he hopped to other settlements.

"I'll take ye to me house," Antrina told him. "Right now there's no place else we kin go that'll be safe. We kin finger out a better place for ye efter that. But fer now we jus gotsta git offer dese roads."

She swerved into a wheeling cluster of trucks as large as the first. They loomed like canyon walls around the yellow Faravan. It bobbed on the furious current. When at last Antrina scooted beside another roving taxi that was caught in the cluster, a Faravan like her own, it seemed as though her car had entered sunlight. She left it. She pushed her vehicle between more hulking, hurtling trucks in blinking succession. The landscape around them opened wider. Darby watched the gaps elongate between the vehicles they passed: truck, truck, taxi, truck, taxi, taxi, truck, truck, truck.

They drove for a longer span than Darby had ever before spent inside an automobile. He drooped. He felt dispirited. He felt isolated, dispossessed, separated from every elaborate edifice that anchored his identity. His chest, arms, neck and back remained concealed, although no one ambled nearby to see the skin ads even if they showed. The scene outside looked desolate. The populous sidewalks had disappeared where the connector began. The familiar street-side shops and offices and such had vanished a far distance back. Now only stark, green slopes filled the vista outside the speeding car. At least the remote, disconsolate landscape had appeared far off when he viewed it from the broad connector. When the cab suddenly veered away, the treed, unpeopled hills closed tightly around Darby. On the smaller, slower road, the encroaching tangle seemed ready to collapse upon the car. Darby had never been inside a preservation zone before. Antrina's constant chatter became his only, vague respite.

"Maybe ye kin make some kind uf a deal wid em," she said. "Maybe efter ye wait some days ye kin talk to em an mebbee mek some kind uf a deal wid em. Efter all, ye de slugger. Ye de big star. Ye de hero uf ev-body. They-ill mek a deal wid ye efter ye let em cool down fer a bit."

The road looked ready to disappear in the darkness inside a low curve up ahead.

"Ye kin be safe at me house fer some days," she told him. "They woan come fer ye there. They woan come on the Reservation. Even if they thin yer there, even if they finger out that ye come home wid me, they woan come on the Reservation te git ye. Ye-ill be safe at me home fer some days til dey cool down fer a bit. Then ye kin finger it out. Then ye kin make some kind uf a deal wid em."

Darby felt sudden relief when he saw the dense forest break up past the curve. A clearing ran perpendicularly up the slope outside his car window. It was cultivated, with rows of low plants that stepped like alternating stripes on the hillside. High above, at the end of a drive that led upward along one edge of the field, he made out a house or a building or barn. It was green itself. At least part of the building was green. Large, hexagonal patches of white blocked around small windows that appeared to be scattered in a random arrangement upon the building's walls.

"We on the Reservation now," said Antrina. "We'll be okay here. We'll be to me house rel soon now."

Further along he saw other clearings, planted like the first with carefully tressed stalks and vines and low-clinging bushes, spaced and sequenced to create rows of texture and color that tumbled upward toward lone buildings at the top. One building was painted in stripes, made from alternating bands of green and yellow that colored the slats that sided the structure. Another was a solid, golden color, done neatly, with brisk, crisp outlines of blue around its door and its windows. The clearings grew closer. Above the tiered, living fields Darby saw buildings painted red and orange and blue. Two wore big accents in the yellow color that appeared to be a favorite.

Finally the forest vanished altogether. The houses stood nearer, clustered on lots that ran adjacent to each other. They were colored the same candy hues, painted yellow and orange and blue and red like the buildings that had topped the clearings, most with similar, bold, fracturing contrasts that gave gay relief to windows and doors and on one house created a paisley design upon a blank wall. Antrina rolled her car into a short drive that stopped at the front of a red-painted house that was blotched where big scabs of paint had fallen away.

"It's called resinite siding," she said in explanation. "My Antro wanted it cause it's spost te last ferev. But it only come in white. Who wan a white house? I wan a red house so my Antro painted it red. But we lernt that paint doan stick to resinite siding. Now we lose a lit bit more paint ev time we get a storm."

Darby climbed hesitantly out of the car. He eased down his feet fearing that the ground might take his steps differently. He scurried around the car to catch up with Antrina, who was already ascending the three cropped steps that led up to a yellow door. He rushed up the stairs right behind her. But when he stepped inside the house he felt the door wave and flap awkwardly as he tried to pull it closed. He had to stop and turn around and guide the door more carefully into its jamb. A hinge was broken loose. By the time he faced back into the house, Antrina had walked deeper inside. He couldn't see where she had gone. He felt the taint of trespass as he stepped through the kitchen where he guessed she had passed. He turned into a hallway. Its walls gloamed in darkness. He turned again. He stopped smack behind his housekeeper. She was standing inside a living room in the front on the house.

An angular, untidy man lay stretched out full-length on a couch across the room. He had been sleeping. He sat up abruptly when Darby appeared behind Antrina. He looked startled, uncomprehending. He rubbed his eyes with his open palms. An old-style television played noisily in the room.

"We hedda come here," Antrina said over its din. "We hedda git offer the roads right away."

The man blinked at her from the couch, comprehending just dimly. He struggled to focus his eyes on Darby, who rose head and shoulders above Antrina as he stood behind her.

"The blue men were efter us both," she stated emphatically. "Efter what haped, they would of taked us both. An evne if they taked only one of us, if they taked only me er if they taked only him, ye wouldne have en-thin left. So we hedda git offer the roads. We hedda come here cause there woan ne place else to go."

When the man recognized Darby at last, his eyes darted downward as his head fell away in an impulse of avoidance. After he gathered himself, he glanced up again with a glare that showed sullen discomfort and also disdain. He scowled. Darby looked back at him blankly. The man rose and brushed past Darby as he left the room. He tried to dash a chilly glance at the athlete but he could not sustain it as he passed. His eyes drooped once again. He skulked away brooding. Antrina followed him out of the room. Darby found himself uncomfortably alone again.

He stepped deeper into the living room to avoid overhearing their argument. The rattling little television droned over their voices. Ned Instead spoke earnestly from the small, fussy box. Looking down at the screen, Darby saw his own picture imposed behind the ordinary grimace of Instead. The altered aspect of his image made him gape. Darby had grown so accustomed to seeing himself on the vid that the big, blazoned, screen personation had become his own, personal self-image. But seen on this feckless little television, sputtering and shaking with unsubstantial fury, his picture looked cramped and distant. It gave up its immediacy. It gave up its authority. Darby could look away from the picture as easily as he might choose to look toward it.

The screen cut away to a clip showing Darby miss the ball during the big game two days earlier. It was the first time he had seen a replay showing the error. The slugger blushed with embarrassment and regret. As his flub replayed a second time Instead spoke over the action: ". . . has turned up evidence of a willful conspiracy to lose . . .."

Antrina returned.

"That's my Antro," she announced to Darby. She gestured with her head toward the interior of the house. "He woan bother you. Ye kin jus stay way from him if ye want. I doan care. He's always been jealous of you en-way. I think you pay me too much money. You pay me so much that he doan heffta work. I tell him he kin git a job en-way, even if he doan make as much as me make, cause we kin always use extra. But he doan like it if he mek less then me. It's not yer fault. I tole him that. He should be thanks that I make so much. But he doan listen to me. I doan care if you doan even talk to him."

Darby had scarcely heard a word. Antrina followed his eyes to the television. "Oh," she said when she saw Darby's image ahead of the solemn narration. The cramped little television showed his skin advertisements. It showed the slow pirouette Darby turned whenever he came up to bat, with his arms held aloft while one hand raised the scuffed blue club that, like his chest, bore the imprint of Pepsi-Coke. The vid's motion was slowed, with the image of Darby zoomed in to show the body ads up close, while the voice of Ned Instead hummed distantly: ". . . his sponsors denounce . . .."

*Pepsi-Coke*, emblazoned and shining across Gab Darby's oiled pectorals, lilted across the tight little sandy screen.

". . . pick him out by his body ads . . .."

*Colonel Chicken* in black letters shone crisply within a band of yellow around the vid figure's neck.

". . . can't be covered up . . ."

*K-Wal Stores* ran up the man's arm.

". . . or completely hidden . . ."

*Corolla* slanted in a diagonal white stripe across his broad back.

". . . If you see him . . .," went Instead inside the imperious little box.

The news-talker's narration penetrated Darby like a palpable buzz beneath his scalp. He felt unaccountably separated from the illustrated figure inside the chattering box. The small man called Gab Darby inside the vid, crammed into a close-up view, contained, hemmed, bordered and framed within the flickering appliance across the room, could have been anyone. It might have been no one. It was impermanent, fickle, indefinite, ready to scatter forever into luminous fuzz.

## CHAPTER SEVEN

Adjunct General Nelson Pierce did not want his face to appear brooding when he looked into the vid that connected him to his superiors. But he couldn't figure out how to control his expression without making it look even more contorted. Most of all he just wanted them to speak. Make a noise. If they said something, anything, he could count on his reply to mask the uncomfortable leer he felt pulling at his lips.

At last President Jeannie Welk-Emerson-Landose blurted, "where did they all come from?"

"They didn't come from anywhere," General Pierce replied, meting his words in order to keep his composure. "They didn't have to come here. They're already here. This is their home. They're here all the time. They just came out. From what we've been able to ascertain, there was no garrison or encampment or anything like that. This was not an organized unit. Well, let me take that back. This was a very well organized unit.

And well trained. But it was not a single, permanent command. It was more like a militia." Pierce recognized that his explanation was uncharacteristically long. But he went on anyway, not from any eagerness to speak; more from a fear that the conversation would lull to silence again if he stopped.

"From what we have ascertained, the word was somehow spread that we were coming out. They knew we were coming out and they had time enough to prepare. Time enough to gather their men together and be waiting for us. Be waiting for us first at Plixinar, then at Banth."

"They were waiting for you," President Welk-Emerson-Landose exclaimed at Pierce through the vid. A vertical line split the general's screen. One side showed the President. The other side carried the image of First Adviser Mel Santee. Instinctively the general snapped his eyes to the side of the screen that carried the President's image.

"Yes, ma'am," he replied. "They appeared to be well prepared and waiting for us."

"Why would you go out there if they were waiting for you?" she demanded, though the question seemed more an exclamation of surprise and astonishment. And censure, too.

"We never expected the high level of resistance we encountered, ma'am. Besides, you ordered us to go there. It came from the plan I originally drew up. Which you approved. You wanted us to seize this person you call Vestin. And you wanted us to do it with a real show of force. That's why we went over-land. Our objective was very clear. We identified the house he was staying in. It was out in Plixinar. Some friends or supporters were putting him up there. We marched out to seize him, as you ordered. You saw this whole plan in advance. And approved it. The only problem was, they somehow knew we were coming.

This Vestin—his actual name appears to be Jantillus Flavin—he was gone by the time we arrived. And a pretty well equipped cadre was there to greet us."

"But that was in Plixinar," broke in First Adviser Santee. Pierce shifted his eyes to Santee's split of the vid screen. "You said that was in Plixinar that you went to get Vestin. But you said before that the fighting was in Banth."

"That's right, Mr. Santee. As I reported, the fighting began in earnest in Banth. That's where the actual battle took place. Well, at least that's where it began. This encounter in Plixinar was just a skirmish. Hardly any shooting at all. Even the news talkers would have stayed to witness that one—if we had let them come along in the first place. You'll recall that I already told you that. I said that our first encounter with the Bortonese occurred in Plixinar. That was our first destination. That's where we expected to seize Jantillus Flavin. And that was only a small exchange. The militia there dispersed very quickly. According to my commander's assessment, he didn't think they had the belly for a fight. He took no casualties. He inflicted only two, three, on the enemy at the most. Then they dispersed."

"Then how did you end up in Banth," Santee demanded.

"That was a command decision, Mr. Santee," said General Pierce to the screen. "My field commander had been left with the option to move on to Banth if circumstances warranted. He reported in after the engagement in Plixinar. He reported light resistance. He reported that Jantillus Flavin, or Vestin, or whatever his name is, had fled and could not be seized. Therefore I told him that he should therefore move on to Banth. We had to have something to crow about. That was part of your orders too. The Bortonese were keeping a large weapons cache in Banth. We knew that for certain. Since we had failed to take Jantillus

Flavin, and since Captain Endright had encountered such light resistance, I gave him the go-ahead to move on and seize the weapons. That way, at least we would salvage something from the operation. We just never expected so many of them to be assembled at Banth."

"So many!" shrieked the President. General Pierce's eyes snapped back to her side of his screen. "How many could there be? How many did they need? You're supposed to be the best army in the world. How could you get beat like that by a little militia!"

"I wouldn't underestimate them, ma'am," said the general gravely. "Don't misunderstand that because I call them a militia, that they were in any way rag-tag or unprofessional. This was a well-trained and determined fighting force. They may not have worn uniforms, but those were good soldiers that met Captain Endright on the field. Far better than your intelligence had indicated. I've reviewed the battle videos very carefully. You should have too by now. At Banth the captain followed very sound pre-emptive measures. He was in the process of securing a unit-wide perimeter before moving in to seize the munitions cache. It appeared lightly guarded, but he still was taking every approved precaution. His troops had disembarked from the protective transporters, from the PT personnel carriers. He was in the process of dispatching his troops to secure all the necessary, protective access points. The primary one was a small bridge. It was a principal access point into the village. Our platoon had just about reached it when the main body of the enemy force was seen descending the hill on the other side of the bridge. They appeared well armed. They came down in combat array. Very orderly. To tell you the truth, I think they were just as surprised to see us as we were to see them. But they responded very quickly. Captain Endright gave the order for the bridge to be destroyed, but the enemy fired on the platoon before they could carry it out. They had good cover, they had superior numbers, and they knew what they were doing. They drove the platoon off the bridge and back to our main position. Then the enemy secured the bridge themselves. They crossed it and arrayed themselves in a secure position opposing ours. They had good cover. They appeared to be well armed. And they were very determined."

"I still don't get why he didn't have any Clintons with him," blurted Santee. "He could have just blown them away."

"The operation was designed for speed and stealth. It was a small-scale reconnaissance, Mr. Santee. We didn't want to risk any of the control and coordination problems we've encountered with the remotely operated Clinton battle tanks. We felt that they would have compromised the mission."

"But the Clintons could of just blown em away."

"The situation developed very quickly, Mr. Santee. And after they crossed the bridge, the enemy was in very close proximity. The Clintons haven't been shown to be effective at close range. That's when the coordination and control problems occur."

"But at least there's no one inside them," shot back President Welx-Emerson-Landose. "You wouldn't have lost so many of our troops if you had used the Clintons."

Pierce remained silent.

"And I still don't get why you didn't get back inside the protective transporters," said Santee. "Why didn't you just retreat inside the PT vehicles? Maybe you wouldn't of lost so many that way, either."

"In my estimation we would have taken more casualties,

Mr. Santee. Remember, the enemy had Skeeters. They would have taken out the personnel carriers wholesale, with everyone inside of them. That's why we couldn't evacuate with the birds, either. The sortie never would have reached them. We tried sending them in. We lost two. The Skeeters took them down. The birds had to turn around and come back. In my estimation, Captain Endright's decision to return on foot was the best decision he could have made. It was better to take them on with small arms. The Skeeters are some of our best weapons. They're deadly against mechanization. They're deadly against aircraft. That's what they were designed for . One man can fire it as easily as a rifle and it will take out practically anything."

"What the hell are they doing with them?" snapped the President.

"They got them from us," replied General Pierce crisply. On his screen, the heads of the President and her First Adviser turned, indicating that they exchanged glances where they sat together inside the meeting room at the President's offices back home.

"I can't emphasize enough how determined those fighters were," said Pierce, worrying as he spoke if they might discern his rising anger through the filter of the vid. "Central Intelligence reported just the opposite. Based on their reports, I never expected this high level of resistance. I never expected that they would harry us the way they did all the way along our withdrawal route. I never expected them to be so well armed. I never thought they'd have Skeeters. In fact, the reports we received from you specifically stated that they did not have Skeeters."

Santee and the President exchanged another glance.

"The action might have ended a lot worse," General Pierce went on. "But I dispatched a company of Marines along with a couple of old Abrams. The Marines sent squads out in front to keep the Skeeters away from the tanks. That's easier to do when you only have a couple of them. They reached Plixinar just before Captain Endright made it back there from Banth. By then his unit was almost in a full rout. The Abrams helped scatter the enemy. They held them off, at least. With the Marines we were able to make it back. Otherwise, I think it would have ended a lot worse."

"What are you doing now," said Santee in the vid.

"I have a lot of reconnaissance out. On foot, out in the bush and in the jungle. We're intelligence-gathering in the towns and villages, too. I need to know what we're up against. I won't dispatch any more units until I have a realistic appraisal of what we're up against."

"Aren't you going after Vestin again?" prodded Santee.

"One of the things we're trying to determine right now is who their leaders are. At the moment we know very little about their command structure. We know very little about anything. How many there are. Who's leading them all. If they have permanent units or if they're all militia. Where they might be hiding. We don't know any of that. Right now I can't even tell you for certain who organized the attack at Plixinar and Banth."

"But what about Vestin?" repeated Santee.

"From what we've been able to ascertain, there is nobody named Vestin. If it's Jantillus Falvin you mean, he doesn't seem to have been anywhere near Plixinar or Banth. At least not when we were there. From the intelligence we've gathered, he fled well before we even reached Plixinar and he was nowhere in the area when the fighting began."

"But we need you to get Vestin," the adviser demanded.

"I can get this Vestin fellow you're after," replied General

Pierce. "I can get anyone. I can do anything you order me to do. But I'd be a fool to move out of garrison again until I have an accurate appraisal of our adversaries."

After General Pierce signed off, after the big screen on the President's meeting-room wall flicked luminously white, then faded to blank matte and blended, after they heard the security prompt tell them that the video call was fully disconnected, that they were alone and unobserved, that all of the room's communication gear securely was locked off, President Jeanie and her First Adviser remained silent for a moment longer. Santee, for his part, waited for the President to speak first.

"Where'd they get the missiles?" she asked at last, almost sadly.

"I don't know," said Santee. "I mean, they must have got em from us. But I don't know how. I mean, Bortus has all the Skeeters. His army does. We made sure of that when we sold em. I don't know how the fuck those peasants could of got their hand on em. They're fucking no-goods. They're just a fucking bunch of trailer trash. Central Intelligence made sure the missiles were in the hands of Bortus's army. I saw the report. They made sure of it."

"But this is Bortus's army."

"Well, yeah, kinda, but not anymore. I mean, these are just all the deserters and stuff. This isn't the real army. The real army is supposed to have all the weapons. These guys just have their guns and stuff like that. Little stuff. I don't see how they could of got the missiles—if they really have 'em. I'll find out. I'll get to Central Intelligence right away and have em find out."

"What are we supposed to do now?" mused the President hopelessly.

"This is all Pierce's fault," Santee shot back. "That's the way

I see it. He's the one who didn't get Vestin. He's the one that went on to Banth. We never said anything about that in your orders I doan care what he says. And he should of sent out the Clintons. None of this would of happened if he'd sent out the Clintons in the first place."

"But Pierce doesn't have to explain it all. It's me that's got to go on the vid and explain it all."

"And it looks to me like this Vestin is a lot bigger then we ever thought before. This is a lot more than a little ambush like before. This was a regular battle. He must have more troops, more power. I think you can let the people know that we're up against a real power-house here. He's bigger than Sadam was. He's way bigger than bin Laden. It's all because of this Vestin. You've got to drive that home. He's the villain. He's attacking our men and women. He's killing our soldiers. It'll be real easy to get all the people really stirred up against him."

"I can't believe we lost so many."

"That was Pierce's fault. I don't think you'll have to take any of the blame for that."

## CHAPTER EIGHT

The makeshift game relieved Darby's lingering discomfort. The hilltop was bare, the houses were out of view, and the skuffed dirt ballfield was a lot like the place where he had played when he was a boy. The children were much the same too. Darby played on the girls' team, to even the sides. He wore the baggy black shirt from Antrina, which helped him to vaguely match the girls all around him, although their shirts were party colored: orange, yellow, red and some just a bedazzling white made to sparkle by bleaching. Their opponents, the boys, wore no shirts at all, showing narrow shoulders, lean backs and spindly chests turned nutty brown by the sun's warm benevolence. The boys stood arrayed around the field. The girls, with Darby, clustered on the side, for another turn at bat.

Darby stepped up to bat first. He tapped the ball carefully, hitting the first throw even though it was an errant pitch. The ball arced just over the reach of the leaping infielders, landing on the shag just beyond them and then putting on a long roll that split between the two sprinting boys in the outfield, who threw down their fielder's gloves so they could dash after it unencumbered, flailing their arms and huffing and shrieking in excited frustration as they raced toward the skidding ball. Darby started around the bases at half speed. When he rounded the first base—with the two zooming outfielders still only closing on the ball as it rolled—another boy threw down his glove and jumped piggy-back style onto Darby back to slow the big man. Other boys ran to join in, nodding their heads and beating the air with spindly arms and churning their feet in the dirt as they powered toward Darby. He let them pounce, laughing as they smacked against him like blown papers, laughing as they clutched both his legs and as they pulled on his arms. He dragged them along, five shrieking, hollering boys. He lumbered. He towered. At last he let them topple him. He fell carefully, easing down his great bulk to avoid hurting any of the boys. Other boys raced to pile on. The girls from Darby's team ran out too, protesting shrilly that the boys were playing unfairly. The girls jumped and screamed and reached into the scrum to pull at ankles and arms to disentangle their teammate.

At last the slugger rose powerfully from the pile. He shrugged away the boys. They grinned and laughed and slapped their thighs happily as they dispersed, charmed and aglow.

"Ei gew gin," Darby announced. "Ei gew gin. Ye no nee kin teclee de hetter."

"He hits again. He hits again," the girls cheered as they skipped and hopped all around him. They escorted Darby en-masse to the side. But before he bent to pick up his bat again he saw Antrina climb suddenly into view, scurrying hen-like up the bare little hillside that lead to the ballfield. Her sister, Lunite, hustled beside her, and as the two women drew close Antrina waved to Darby and called to him: "Gabdubby, Gabdubby, ye have to come in right away. Right now. Ye hefte hurry en come in wid us."

Darby stepped unhesitantly away from the claque of young girls who had grown suddenly still from the grave interruption. The two women stopped to wait for him, panting unevenly to recapture their breath. When Darby reached them he did not break step. Antrina and Lunite synched into stride at his sides, the three hustling abreast down the hill toward the red spotted house. Antrina stopped and turned back toward the children. She pushed both her hands toward them in a gesture that seemed meant to hold them away—though the children remained standing upon the field, dumbstruck, clustered, brightly colored, befuddled, their arms dangling uncertainly at their sides.

"Doan follow us," Antrina shouted at them. "Keep playin. Ye keep playin jus lik noth happed jus now."

When she turned back toward her house she had to run to catch up to Darby and to Lunite, her sister.

"We just heard from over at Sally Flats," Antrina sputtered between gulps for breath. "They had the helicopters there and they sayed it looked like they were coming over the hills te us here. We cant let em see ye here."

The loud, percussive hammer-slap of the rotors arrived just as Darby reached for the door handle. He tugged but the door hung up: the damn broken hinge. Darby had to carefully push it back into the door jamb in order to reseat it evenly. In a burst three helicopters cleared the dimpled hill at the settlement's far end. Darby had to pull the door handle slowly, with deliberate care, supporting the weight of the door as it opened.

The clap stepped up to a roar as the beating machines soared toward the house. When the door was gapped open just enough to allow it, Darby slipped inside. The women pushed in at his heels, crowding Darby toward the center of the floor of the kitchen.

He looked down at the table where four people sat. They didn't look back. Instead the people stared blankly ahead, listening rather than watching. They listened to the helicopters dart rapidly over the house. The machines paused. They banked upward toward the playing field where the children remained. They hovered there. They scatted a further notch off. They waited. They pushed on again. Their whirring receded. It vanished.

"What do you think?" a woman asked quietly from down at the table. "Do you think that they left now?"

"It sounded to me like they flew off toward Rinkers Bert," said an earnest looking man. "Did they see you?" he asked Antrina with grim urgency.

"No," she replied. "I don't think they saw us at all. They were still on the other side of the house when I got in the door. I was the last to get in. They couldn't see me at all through the house."

"Why did they come?" asked the first woman, a big, startled-seeming frau.

"I don't know," said the earnest man. "Maybe they came just to scare us. Just to show that they're not going to leave us alone anymore. Or maybe they came because they thought Gab Darby is here and they wanted to look for him. It doesn't matter anymore why they came. It just goes to show what I'm saying: It's not safe for him to stay here anymore."

Antrina said, "Gabdubby should sit down first. Then we

can start into everything."

Obligingly he sat in an open chair at the table. Antrina lowered herself into the last remaining seat. The earnest man, who was the only man among the six Bortos in the kitchen, stood up so that Lunite, the sister, could use his seat. A rising aroma of coffee burnished the air.

"We didn't know they were coming here," Antrina began. "We all got together to talk to you and just when I started to make the coffee we heard from Sally Flats that the helicopters were coming. That's when we went up to get you just in time. Who finished up the coffee?" she asked the group.

"I finished making it," said the earnest man.

"Did you put enough water in?" Antrina demanded. Then, to Darby, she offered, "he likes it too strong, so he always puts in not enough water."

"I did," the man answered, "I put it all in."

She pushed a ready-made cake in a flop-topped box toward the table's center. "Everybody's got to take some of this," she announced. Dimly, from the living room, came the unmistakable tone of news-talking on the vid, sounding self-infatuated even from the rattling little box that Antro always watched. In the lull in the kitchen the people keyed their ears to its buzzing narration.

"All the sudden everything is different now," Antrina announced to Darby. "It's different from only two days ago when you just got here. They started some big fighting now in Bortinca. We don't know too much about it yet. We're just finding out about it today. But it's real serious this time. It's going to make everything a lot different for us who are living here now. It's going to make everything a lot harder. We don't know how for sure. But my friends and my neighbors here, they all came here today to talk about it. And to tell me that they don't think it's safe for you to stay here anymore. It's not safe for you and it's not safe for me. Because now, with the way things are going in Bortinc, if they put two and two together they might come looking for you here. Maybe that's even what those helicopters are all about today. I don't know. But it's true now that they might come here now to take you and that would be bad for both of us."

"It's what you call a worse case scenario," elaborated the earnest man, who now stood at the counter overlooking the table. "Because we really don't know yet for sure what's going to happen. But I think it's safe to say that they might stop respecting Reservation rules. They have an excuse to do that now, with the fighting that's getting going over there and everything. So now they might be able to come here to take you without anybody to complain about it. I think yesterday you were safe here but today I don't think you're safe here anymore at all."

"I think today it's going to be bad for us just because we're Bortono," said Lunite, the sister, a squat, rotund woman with hands chaffed and cracked from the solvents she used in the restaurants she scrubbed. "Yesterday it was better for you to be here if you were. Now, I think, just the opposite. All the sudden it's different now cause the fighting is different. Now it's a lot worse."

"It's different now because now we're fighting Americans," explained the standing man. "Before we were just fighting the soldiers that Bortus sent out. They were our own soldiers and when they came out to bother us we would just send them back. But this time they weren't Bortus's soldiers that came out. This time they were real American soldiers. We did the same thing: we came out and just sent them back. But this time it wasn't just

Bortus's men we were fighting."

"Everybody has to eat this," said Antrina as she nudged the puff cake deeper onto the table. "If you leave it here I'll eat it all. The coffee is ready now. Have it with some coffee."

"It might be that we're over-reacting," the man went on gravely. "It might be that nothing here will change all too much. But I got pretty worried. I think that we need to prepare for the worse."

"Lunite," commanded Antrina, "Lunite, get the coffee."

"Wait a minute," interrupted a woman at the table. She held out her hand for attention. "Wait a minute. I think they're saying something now. On the TV."

The six Bortonese keyed their ears to the distantly buzzing dictation that came from the vid.

"Antro," boomed Antrina, "Antro, turn up the sound. Turn it up loud so we can hear it in here."

Ned Instead chirped, his tone prefatory and slightly hushed to subdue its scintillation as he declared that the President was joining him now, exclusively, to tell him secrets that she had not shared with any of the other news talkers.

"Now here's the latest," he said. The sound entered the room like a distant holler. The six in the kitchen canted their heads to hear it more clearly. "President Jeanie," went Instead, "thank you for taking the time to visit with us during this difficult crisis."

"You're welcome, Ned. You know that I always feel that it's very important to keep everybody up to the minute, and I certainly appreciate the job you and all of your colleagues do to help us get the truth out to people."

"The love-fest," mocked a woman at Antrina's table.

"Have there been any recent developments you can share

with us now?" asked Instead.

"Well, there haven't been any more attacks against our peace-keepers. I can tell you that. That's because right away I ordered them to take defensive action. As soon as we got word of the escalating conflict, I ordered our, uhm, our troops to take every action they needed to protect their own safety. Their safety is my number one concern. Just like always"

"Do you anticipate more attacks?"

"Right now we're assessing the situation. Central Intelligence is on the scene right now and they're working very hard to gather all the information we need. Let me assure you that we're being very careful, very, very careful to find out exactly what we're up against. Most of all, we want to assure the safety of our, our, of our, ah, peacekeepers over there."

"What about the attacks at Plixnar and Banth?" asked Instead. "Do you have any more information on who's responsible?"

"Antro," hollered Antrina, "Antro, turn it up more."

"We have very little information that I can give out to you right now," blared the voice of the President. "Obviously there's a lot that I know that I can't tell you, because I don't want to compromise our mission. And I especially don't want to jeopardize the safety of our, uhm, soldiers. I especially don't want to do that. But I can tell you that we're doing everything possible, absolutely everything possible to bring the rebels that are responsible to justice."

"Does that include the rebel leader Vestin, President Jeannie?"

"Well, I can tell you that we've been chasing Vestin since right after the ambush at Dink. And I can tell you that he was in the vicinity when our army got attacked at Plixinar and Banth."

"Are you saying that Vestin is responsible for these most recent attacks too, President Jeanie?"

"Well, like I said, Ned, there's some things I just can't tell you right now."

In the kitchen the earnest man said, "this Vestin they keep talking about, nobody knows who he is. I don't know anybody who even heard of the name before."

"Shush," shot the stout frau. "I want to hear this."

"How was he able to inflict so many casualties?" asked the voice of Instead.

"We're looking over some of the command decisions made at the time of the battle, at the time of the attacks at Plixinar and Banth. We don't have a complete picture yet, Ned, but we're looking to see if maybe our field command maybe went too far. Maybe it overstepped its authority."

"Are you talking about mistakes made by the American commanders?"

"Let me just say that there's not even a good reason why our people were even in the town of Banth at the time of the attack. That wasn't spelled out in their original orders. I never sent them to Banth. I can assure you of that. I can assure you that we're doing everything we can to find out why our fighters were put in harms way like that."

"Do you think you might change commanders?"

"I can't say anything about that right now, Ned. I don't want to say anything that might jeopardize the safety of our, ah, our guys."

"Can you tell us anything about what kind of mistakes that were made?"

"No. I can't, Ned. Not really. It's still too early. I mean, like I said, we don't have the whole picture yet. But it looks like maybe our people were sent out without enough protection. Like the big weapons. Like, maybe if they had had some of the big weapons with them, maybe then they could have defended themselves better."

"What about sky power?" asked Instead with a knowing air.

"Well, Ned, as you know, we're very, very careful about when to use the full destructive force of sky power. You know that we're very careful to make sure that we fully evaluate its impact on the environment before we go ahead with any kind of an air assault. I very much respect the important process of environmental impact assessment, and I respect the work of all of the people who participate in those assessments."

"But even without the air power, are you saying that our soldiers were unprepared?"

"Our soldiers weren't unprepared. We have the best soldiers in the world. There's no question about that. I want to be perfectly clear about that. Our soldiers are always prepared. But maybe their commanders sent them out without the big weapons. You know: Clinton tanks and other big weapons like that, that they needed."

"That's astounding, President Jeannie. We heard earlier, during the press conference by General Pierce, that the rebels were very well trained and very well equipped. But you're saying that our side was, under-, well, was under-equipped."

"We believe so, yes."

"That's astounding. Do you think they might have won if they were better equipped? If they had these big weapons you're talking about?"

"Yes, Ned. It's possible."

"That's astounding, President Jeannie. Now, to your

knowledge, have to told this to anyone before now?"

"No, Ned. To my knowledge I don't think so."

"President Jeannie, I know we're running short of time here, but I just want to take a moment to remind our viewers that this is an exclusive, live interview with President Jeannie Welk-Emerson-Landose. Now, President Jeannie, one thing I'm sure we're all wondering about is the service men and the service women who were killed. Can you tell us anything about what's being done for their families, and what arrangements are being made for them?"

"We're having all the families flown here . . .," began the President, but the serious-minded man in the kitchen cut in, addressing Darby directly.

"It's not that we want to fight America or anything like that," he explained. "We feel like we're a part of America already, like we're all the same, cause we've come and gone so freely for so long back and forth. But when you sent the Peacekeepers there—you call them Peacekeepers but to us they are just soldiers. In Borto we don't like it that there's suddenly so many American soldiers there just to back up Bortus. Because Bortus doesn't do anything for us. When he doesn't like the laws of the legislature, he gets rid of the legislature. He dissolves it. He declares it is defunct and he sends them home. Then he just makes the laws himself."

From the living room the television still droned: ". . . a memorial service is going to be held at the Smithsonian . . ."

"And he makes men join his army. Because of course with the army he can get away with things like ignoring the legislature. So you have to join his army or go in jail. That's why I came here. That's why a lot of us came here. In the army you have to leave your home, and then you have nothing to do except sometimes you go out and bother other people. Sometimes you bother your own neighbors. I thought, if I had to leave home, I might as well come here."

"... giving them full hero's honors ... "

"And now people have to make room in their houses for your tourists to sleep there."

"... which they deserve ..."

"And because people don't like that, and they don't want to pay for Bortus' palace and his houses and all his rich things with the taxes that he makes, then America sends your army to help him out."

"Quiet," snapped the big woman at the table. "I can't hear what they're saying."

Instead spoke more: "Is there anything to some of the speculation we've heard that now we might see an American pull-out from Bortinca?"

"Absolutely not," answered the President. "We're the best country in the world. We can't let other people push us around. This is an attack on America's pride. I'll never allow that, and I know the American people are behind me one hundred percent. We have a lot of interests to protect. Bortus, the President of Bortinca, is one of our all-time biggest supporters. We have to stand by him. And think of all the rain forest over there. We don't think it will be safe in the hands of the rebels. They want to destroy the rain forest. Think of the children. If we don't stop the rebels, our children will grow up never knowing what a rain forest is. Then there's our sponsors. They have their businesses there. Those are all good American companies that employ a lot of good Americans. But most of all I'm thinking about our, our, ahm, ahb, about our men and women in uniform. I won't have a rebel leader attacking them. I won't stand for it, and I know the people of America won't stand for it either. Before I even talk about any kind of a pull-out, I'm going to see to it that everyone responsible for this is brought to justice."

"Thank you, President Jeannie," said Instead. As he slid into a wrap up, as he announced that Vid News Analyst Little George would now join him to discuss what the President had just discussed, the big frau at the table intoned, "here it comes: the love-fest." Antrina boomed out, "Antro, Antro, you can turn that thing down now." The standing man resumed his earnest discourse to Gab Darby.

"All this talk about the rain forest," he said. "We lived with the rain forest just fine, but then Bortus came and said we couldn't live there anymore and all the American Peacekeepers came to make sure we couldn't live there. But how come its okay for all the tourists to go there when they want? And we have to let them stay in our houses. And the tourists come and fix our houses for us. When our houses don't need fixing. But they do just little things. They hammer on them and change them and they go to the rain forest to get sun tans and see snakes and then when they leave we have to put our houses back the way they were before they fixed them. They want to paint everything white."

"We don't need to talk about that now," interrupted Antrina.

"I thought he should need," defended the man, "I thought he might need to know everything that's going on over there."

"But there's not time for all the details now," she said. "You always go into all the little details."

"But the details are important," he protested.

"What's important now," she said, "is that Gabdubby know he cannot stay here." She turned to Darby. "I thought it would be okay for you to stay here for longer. I mean, I didn't think anyone would find out. But now, I don't know. Like we been saying and like you can see for yourself by now, I think everything's going to be different now. I think they won't be afraid now to come here to get you. Like the helicopters we saw just now."

"We think the safest place for you to go right now is to Bortinca. I know that might sound crazy to you. But right now we think it is the safest place. Just for now. When everything is finished maybe you can make some kind of deal with them when you come back. But for right now it's not safe for you to stay here anymore and we can't think of anyplace else that's safe but in Bortinc. We all know people there. We all have lots of friends and family and everything like that. We could tell them that you're coming and they could get everything ready for you. With them you'd be safe. You could stay there for a while and you'd be safe from getting turned in or anything like that. I mean, they wouldn't be able to take you and send you back. That's for sure with the way things are happening now. Not anymore. So you'd be safe there. En we come and go all the time. We have ways to get you there that no one knows about. We can get ye there tomorrow if you want."

"You should go tomorrow," said the big woman. "You should go before they come for you. If you're here it will be bad for you and it'll be bad for everyone else too."

"Those helicopters," Antrina said, "who knows when they might come back. Who knows if maybe they'll land the next time and soldiers will come out."

"The army doesn't always do what the video people say the army is doing," explained the earnest man.

"There's already a lot of people like you in Bortinc right

now," urged Antrina. "Lots of Americans. Lots of em been there for a real long time. It's okay fer ye to stay there fer a bit. Mebee efter a while ye kin come back en mek a deal wid em."

But Darby did not give in to the entreaties. At least he showed now sign of giving in. He remained mute. He maintained an unmoved posture while the pleading went on inside the kitchen. Finally, when the others packed off to their separate homes, when Darby and Antrina sat alone at last with only dried coffee rings and the cake half consumed upon the table, she said to him, "I understand how you might not want to talk when all of them are sitting here. But now they're gone en just me alone I have to tell ye that evvy-thin we just say is true. Ye kin stay here if ye wan. I woan throw ye out. But it's better fer ye if ye go. It's better if ye go right now. Es soon es ye kin. I thin they'll come en take ye now. When we came here we had no place else left to go. I thought yeed be safe here, cause I thought they-id nev bother us here. But now all the sudden evvy-thin's changed. I doan feel so safe here now lik I did."

"Ei gew," he said. "Bud erst-a Ei hefta see sum-bod."

"Ye hefta see sum-bod? Ye hefta see um where?"

"Ei gew see um."

"See who?"

"See Ketra."

"See Ketra yer wife?"

"See Ketra."

"She noan yer wife ne-mehr."

"See er."

"Ye can't. Ye canno-ne git te er. She beck in de urb. Ye hef no-ne way te git beck in de urb."

"See er," Darby insisted.

"Ye can't. Ye canno-ne git beck in der urb. I woan tek ye.

Ne-no te see Ketra. I woan tek ye te see er."

"Ei gew me-sel," said Darby.

"Phffft," Antrina scoffed.

"Ei gew. Ei gew me-sel."

"Ye hef no way te git te er."

"Ei gew."

"But why?" she asked him. "I doan git ye. Why go ye te see yer once-wife? Why go ye te see er now? She ne-evvy be yer wife en-more. Ye no-ne see er since ye break. En now ye in de big fight. Ye in de big trouble. Ye hefta git way from here. Ye hefta git way right way. Ye canno-nee git beck in de urb. Ye hef no way te git beck in de urb. I woan drive ye."

"Ei gew."

"But ye hefta git way te Bortinc. Ye hefta git way right way."

"Ei see Ketra. Efta et, efta Ei see de Ketra, den Ei gew te Bortinc."

"Ye mean ye go te Bortinc efta ye see er?"

"Yee."

"Right way efta ye see er?"

"Yee."

"Ye go de same day?"

"Yee."

"Ye go te-mor?"

"Yee, yee, Ei gew te-mor. Efta Ei see de Ketra."

"It's stupid," she said. "I thin it's stupid fer ye te go te de urb jus te see de Ketra. De taker ill be lookin. De takers migh find ye dair. But if ye-ill go te Bortinc, if ye-ill leef fer Bortinc right efta ye see er, then kay."

"Ei gew," said Darby.

# CHAPTER NINE

Partly to ingratiate himself to his American supporters afar, and partially to reassert his own authority at home, Bortus ordered out three tooth-and-nail units of his Domi-Praet Guard, pointing them toward Plixinar and Banth to clean up any faint traces of rebelliousness they might encounter there. He ordered out so many soldiers primarily to assure their success.

But the soldiers did not go. When Bortus learned the following morning that his Guard remained in its barracks in the capital, he summoned his two highest ranking generals, General Frin and General Bieno, to the big hall inside his residence, where routinely Bortus performed deliberations under the eyes of vid-corders. He put on his imperious air as he demanded to know why his soldiers hadn't yet left for the field. Why, he demanded, did it take them so long to get ready?

General Bieno jutted out his chin and replied that of course he did not know. But the question had been meant for General Frin anyway. Bieno—a thick, brutish man with a pugged-up nose and a belligerent air who always rushed to answer every question Bortus put to him—did not command the Domi-Praet Guard. Bieno commanded the Inner-Praet Guard, which had never been ordered out into the field. The Inner-Praet never strayed far from Bortus' residence. It provided the ruler's personal surety.

The Domi-Praet was Frin's command. The Domi-Praet routinely ran out to restore domestic order. For his part, General Frin of the Domi-Praet appeared more confused than forthright. Frin replied that he did not know why his men had not yet motored out. But he would find out right away, he pounded. He would summon all his colonels and majors and captains together at once to find out first hand why the three units orders to Plixinar and Banth had not yet left for the field. He would ask each officer, he said, one at a time, until he felt satisfied that he knew the real reason why the units had not yet left. And if he was not satisfied with the reason, then he would take over and lead the soldiers out of garrison all by himself this time.

But when Frin returned alone to the big hall he brought something less than a satisfactory explanation. He told Bortus, his commander, that his units simply showed no interest in motoring out to attack the citizens of Plixinar and Banth. He said that all of his colonels and majors and captains, almost to a man, had stood coolly indifferent to his demands and his exhortations. Only a few of them had even looked uncomfortable, even when he threatened arrest and dire punishment. Some had clucked at the threat, expressed Frin to Bortus with appropriate outrage. And when he had asked them how they dared to disobey an order from the high commander, his officers seemed only to shrug. One said he would gladly lead out the men, if he had enough men left to lead. Another said it made no sense to lead his men to Plixinar and Banth, because most of his men were already there. And if he led the few that remained in the garrison, the officer had dared to say, he wouldn't return alive. So what did he care about palace threats and exhortations?

Bortus listened silently to Frin's entire, long-running report. He paused with due gravity for a moment without speaking even after General Frin had finally exhausted every word of outrage he could summon. Bortus pursed his lips. He squinted. He creased his brow in deep consternation. At last he said, all right, since Frin's Domi-Praet Guard refused to follow his orders, he would turn to his elite, Inner-Praet Guard to force them. Forget for now about the rebels in Plixinar and Banth, he said to General Frin. Instead go back and tell all of your officers that Bortus is sending his elite Inner-Praets to arrest them all, he said, unless they agree to motor out by this evening to confront the rebels.

General Frin replied that the president's plan was very sound and wise. He said he was certain that the threat of arrest by the Inner-Praets would force the Domi-Praets to follow his order and take to the field. But rather than go himself, he would send his top aide to deliver the ultimatum. He, General Frin, should remain in the large, fortified residence of Premier Bortus, Frin suggested, and await his officers' response from there —although of course he was certain that his officers would respond by complying.

Bortus agreed, commanding Frin to also invite inside the well-fed, well-equipped platoon that always traveled alongside General Frin as his escort. The soldiers could wait more comfortably outside of the heat, in the shaded galleries that lined his compound, said Bortus. At the same time he sent word to General Bieno, commanding him to prepare his Inner-Praet Guards for action against the Domi-Praets—just in case the Domi-Praets still refused to move. The elite Inner-Praet should come out of its garrison right away, Bortus ordered. They should come to his compound and assemble in the streets surrounding the villa. They'd find room, he said, in the streets all around his residence, on every side, where they should wait, well armed, until Bortus issued further orders to General Bieno.

Then Bortus and General Frin waited. From inside the airy residence they anticipated the arrival of Bieno with his brawny armed men. They watched until the sun hung ominously atop the compound's far wall. All the while General Frin could not raise the aide he had sent back to his own Domi-Praet with the ultimatum. Frin tried repeatedly to reach the aide. With each failure, Bortus looked more eagerly for Bieno's arrival. He did not want to summon General Bieno and his Inner-Praet a second time. That would be undignified. But as the day waned and as the evening deadline for the Domi-Praet to finally march out against the rebels drifted past, Bortus hastily placed a second call to General Bieno. Where was Bieno's elite Inner-Praet? It should be circling the residence by now. What was the cause of the delay, the president demanded with scarcely disguised urgency.

Bieno replied that there seemed to be a problem with the Americans. He had called the American garrison next door the instant he had received the original order from Bortus, he said. Naturally he needed the Americans to send along their usual contingent of observers—the company-sized body of well-armed soldiers who routinely ventured out with the Inner-Praets. Of course he would have to bring the observers along, said Bieno, even though his orders had been simply to ring Bortus' residence and await further orders. But the American liaison officer had told Bieno that all American forces had been instructed to stay in their encampments. Bieno didn't know why. He would get to the bottom of it, he assured his commander. He would get an answer very quickly, he insisted. But until he did, and until he had the company of American observers motoring behind him again, the general thought best to keep his elite Inner-Praet Guard inside its own post.

Just after darkness fell that evening, Bortus and General Frin left together for the president's residence in the high country far outside of the capital city. They brought along Frin's well-fed escort, as well as the two-dozen personal men that Bortus kept housed in his palace. They figured they could make it by midnight to the American garrison way up in the hills. From there it would take them only a half hour longer to reach the president's high house.

## CHAPTER TEN

Antrina woke Darby silently. The room was so dark and still that he could not decide if morning had really arrived. She beckoned him to come to the kitchen. The lamp there glared garishly. She gestured toward a layered plait of clothing hung over a chair-back.

"Ye hefte wear these," she said to him. "Listen te what we're gwinteh do. We're gwinteh mek ye look lik yer a Borto. Doan say ye woan. Doan say ye woan-ne wear em. Ye hefta. Listen te whud I'm tellin ye. I talked te me brother gin last nigh. Efter ye tole me ye hefte see de Ketra. I talked te im. Hees always wid good idees bout things lik this. He tole me he thinks es stupid too. He thinks ye ne should-nee go te see de Ketra. But I tole im ye hefte go. He said kay. He said if ye hefte go, he-ill tek ye. He said de best way is fer ye te go wid im. Es better te go wid im den fer me te tek ye in de taxi. He sid he kin get ye inside de homeblock where de Ketra live. Me brother, hees a cleaner. He goes in ev-day wid de cleaning men in his lit-leh truck te clean de homes. He said ef I mek ye look lik yer a Borto, he kin sneak ye in en ye kin see de Ketra en den he kin tek ye way. But ye hefte leef right way. Ye hefte promise me: efter ye see de Ketra, me brother teks ye way right way te get ye outte from here."

"Ei gew," agreed Darby.

"Ye go right way ti-dee?

"Ei gew."

"En ye hefte wear deese," she said to him. "So ye look lik yer a Borto."

He put on a big shirt, like the first, except this one was white. Over it he wore a loose, lightweight jacket that flared down like a bell over his hips and thighs. He wore snug, calf-length pants that were pinked to a scalloped hem high above his ankles. His toes stuck out of canvas-strap shoes.

"I stayed up all nigh to mek em," she told him. "Dint sleep et all. Sewed all the nigh. Cause I knew yewd need em. Ye look lik a real Borto now. I thin yewl fool em wid de way ye look right now. Cept yer so big. Yer so big I hedda mek em, cause I dint have none that-ill fit ye, none I could jus give ye. Hedda mek ev-thin. Cept yer still so big. Ye need te try to look little when ye git te de homeblock. Inside, wid de eyes dat are watchin dere, when ye walk, ye need te stoop down a lit. Bend yer head down so ye doan look so tall."

She reconsidered. "No, no," she said, "doan do that. Walk de same way ye allerways walk. Fergit wud I sid. Jus walk straight up en normal lik. Walk de same way ye allerways walk. Else ye migh look too suspicious, jus in case der watchin de eyes dis time. I doan thin dey will. De eyes, der ev-where. Noan ev really watches wud dey show. Dey hef too many uf um. Caint watch em all. But jus in case, so ye doan look lik yer tryin te hide, walk de same way ye allerways walk. Yewl look cay. En here. Here. Tek dis. Put dis on too. Put on dis hat. It'll hide yer face from de eyes. Jus in case."

The hat was made from panels cut from beer boxes, which were stitched together by a brown, fibrous reed. A wide brim that was woven from the same, cord-like reed flopped down to conceal his face.

"There," said Antrina. "Now ye look like yer a Borto for sure. Now you will be invisible like all the other Borts that go into Ketra's homeblock anytime this morning. Even if they're lookin at their eyes this morning, you'll be okay. No one will notice you. But make sure you don't look at em yourself. I mean, when you're walkin to her door, don't look up at any of the eyes. Keep your head level and straight and walk just the same as you always walk. Just like I've been tellin you. But you have to go now. My brother, Paleo, he's here now. He's outside in his truck. You better go right away. Paleo, my brother, he doesn't like to wait. He doesn't like to be late for anything. But you listen to him. He'll take care. He'll make sure you stay okay. You listen to him good. You have to be very careful."

She turned away her face, concealing it from Darby.

"You promise me that you'll be extra careful," she called to him.

"Ei be," Darby replied.

"You'll do everything Paleo tells you to do."

"Ei do."

The small truck waiting outside wore buffalo horns bossed onto its front. Still, Darby felt like an awkward standout as he walked around to the passenger door, which had been pushed open for him. Not only were his chest, arms and neck fully clad once again. The jacket he wore flared like a window curtain and the hat, he felt, flashed like a beacon.

"Good," said the driver when Darby was inside. "Nobody will look at you when you look that way. I thought it might be a problem because you are so big. It would still be better if you were small. But now I think you'll be okay. I don't think anyone will look at you now. I think what we're doing now is safer when I see how good my sister dressed you."

The driver, Paleo, was the earnest man who had explained so much to Darby inside the kitchen yesterday. At the time Darby had not known he was Antrina's brother.

A man in the truck's second row bent forward and dropped his hand on Darby's shoulder.

"Yer the first time I'm meeting a big baseball hero," the man said to Darby. "That's mostly why I came today. All the others, they chickened out. The fighting in Bortinca made em all stay home. But I came here today to see you. To ride with you. "

"I usually have more workers with me than this," said Paleo. "My crew is usually at least four guys. Plus myself. Usually I have at least four other guys come with me every day. We work separate. We do cleaning at different homes but we all go together to the urb. Today they all decided it was better for them to stay home. But that was because of the fighting. That wasn't because of you."

"Besides," said the man in the back, "I'm supposed to get my money today. I doan care about any fighting that's going on any place. I'm not gonna stay home on a day like today and let anybody keep my money."

"I didn't know all the others would stay," said Paleo. "I didn't know till this morning when I went to pick them up. Now, with so many gone, I think maybe it's a good thing you're coming along with us. Now my truck is more full. Now every-thing looks a little more the way it always looks. Everything looks a little bit more like it's normal."

Paleo left Darby in the underground drive-through below the home-block where Ketra lived. Darby had never visited the place before, though the building was not a great deal different than his own.

"I have to leave you here for one whole hour," Paleo said before he drove off. "If I come back here any earlier than that I think it will look too suspicious for me. But I'll be here in exactly one hour. You should make sure you're waiting for me then. Make sure you're waiting right here where I'm leaving you. In one whole hour exactly. If you're not waiting for me, then I can't stay around here to wait for you. It would be too risky for me."

Darby added the emblems of professional cleaning to his disguise: he strapped a vacuumer to his back, and in one hand he carried a pail weighted with a load of rolled towels, three brushes on handles and two spray bottles, one filled with orange liquid, the other with blue. Moving down the long hallway toward Ketra's door he struggled too hard to appear at ease. Walk normal and upright, Antrina had told him. But how did he normally walk? Avoiding the eyes was easy enough. The cameras were mounted up high, near the ceiling. As long as he held his head level, the wide brim of the hat kept his features obscured. But the walking was hard. How did he ordinarily move his legs and his feet when he walked? It had always been automatic. Who ever thought about how to walk? Do feet move straight forward or do they kick out a little? Do shoulders remain back and straight, or do they sway with each step? Are ordinary strides this long, or maybe they're shorter? The more he thought about it, the harder it became to ape his own rhythm.

The hallway seemed to grow longer. He felt more conspicuous the harder he tried to appear inconspicuous. He felt thoughts themselves interfere with his gait. He felt plodding, clumsy, gawkish, inept. He thought that for sure some monitor watching him through the eyes would pick him out for an impostor. At last he heaved great relief when he reached the door to his former wife's home. He rang her bell. His only desire was to get out of the hallway.

But as the door swung open warily, Darby recalled the question Antrina had put to him in her kitchen the day before: Why go ye te see yer once-wife?

Ketra stood still for an instant. She had aged. The straw-gold hue of her hair looked painted on.

"Well whud de fuck," she uttered. "Dis is de stoopdist thin Ei ev saw. Whud ye doin here? Dis is de last place Ei ev thawet yewd ev come."

Darby stood not knowing what to say.

"Well whud de fuck, yer de cleaner now?" she mocked.

He stared silently.

"Ye look lik yer a fucknin ass hole."

No reply.

"Cumin-on," she said. "Ye bet get yer stoopdist ass in de door afore en-bod sees ye lookin disis way."

Darby stepped in only far enough for Ketra to swing the door closed. He looked around the room warily, unwilling to speak. At last the woman said, "doan worry: Ei doan hef no-ne vid in de rooms uppy here. Ders noan who kin spy-in on me. Noan kin hear whud ye say. De owny vid in dis whole place iss away in de beck. Evne if dey go te git de ov-ride tuh spy onny me, dey canno-nee hear whud Eim sayden uppy here. Course, I got de TV inny me bedroom. But es owny a TV. Es no-ne nee vid. Bud course, deres no-nee de fucknin way yer goin en-where near te insiddy me bedroom.

"Ye kin puddy down de stuff dare," she said to him. "Puddy down dat quewmer, less ye relly plen te clen uppy in here. Puddy it down dere. Siddy self down. Eim a-tellin' ye es iss safe inny me home."

Darby placed the gear on the floor and settled tentatively onto a chair.

"Ei nevne thawet Eid see ye in me homminy here," she said. "Eshly not now wid ev-bod out looknin te take ye. Sheat. Ye cudda come here en time afore ti-dee. Eid a let ye come. Why commy ye here ti-dee? Why commy when dey looknin ev-where te take ye?"

Darby couldn't yet form a reply.

"Ye look lik yer de fuckinny clown. Kin ye relly thik yer foolnin en-bod jus cause ye dress uppy lik dat? Why doan ye tek et uff? Tek et uff righ now. Ei doan evne whan-ne te talky widdy when ye look fucknin dididdy-less lek ye do."

Darby unfastened the buttons that ran down the coat's opening.

"Wendy ye start te wearnin dat fucknin thin?" Ketra asked about the high-collared shirt Darby exposed beneath the jacket. "Ye kin tek et uff too. Ei know whud ye look lie. Ei know who ye elreddy bee. Es no-ne lik ye gosta hide et frommy."

When Darby took off the shirt she said, "Ei allerways sid dose fucknin skin ads wouldda gitty ye kilt. Looky ye et em. Ei betta now ye wiss ye no-ne nev had em on, now wid ev-bod looknin te take ye. Dem ads mek it purdy fucknin hard fer ye te hide, doan dey now, now dat dey gosta ye shewwin aller ovner on de vid, shewwin ev-bod how essy et iss te spot ye. Ye doan relly thik yer gonsta fool en-bod dressied lik ye de fucknin ass hole, de ye? Nonnie dressied lik yer e fucknin boron. Dey probly gonsta throw aller de fucknin borons otter here now en-way. So whiddy ye wansta dressie ewp lik a fucknin boron en-way? Dey gonsta tekky ye ey-way. Dey gonsta tekky ye fer bein a boron er dey gonsta tekky ye fer bein Gadduby."

"Ei gwin way," Darby said to her. I'm going away.

"Ye doan hefte gew," she replied. "Ei doan mean en-thin by whud Ei say te ye. Ei mean, Ei doan mean Ei thik en-bod saw ye er en-thin lik dat. Ei doan thik dey saw ye come here etty all, cause Ei doan thik dey looky too close fer ye here. Ei doan care how many de eyes dey puddy up in de halls. Ev-bod know dat no-bod evne lookies at dose en-way. Dey owny look when dey tryin tuh git sumptin on ye. Dey doan care nuthin bout me and Ei doan thik dey spict ye te commy here. Ei sid te em ye nevne come here en es true. Ye nevne come here afore. De owny time Ei ev saw ye now et all iss when de Wins scewel hass one uf de show dees. Bic fucknin deal. But Ei bet dey watchnin de scewel real close righ now. But Ei doan thik dey watchnin here close et all. Ye nevne ev call me here. Ei tole em dat too. No-ne lik Ei neddy te tell em. Dey knowst et alred. Dey gots aller yer records. Ei know dey gots em."

"Ei mean Ei te gew way far," Darby said. "Far way."

"Whir," she asked him.

"Dey tole mim te no-ne te tell whir te ye."

"Ye mean lik yer gwin te scape?"

"Yee."

"Scape fer real?"

"Yee."

"Bud tuh whir?"

"Dey tole mim te no-ne te tell whir te ye."

"Why no-ne telly me whir?"

"Es relly far way."

"Lik te de nuthner country?"

"Yee."

"Relly de nuthner country?"

"Yee."

"Den how kin ye no-ne telly me whir? Ei gosta know. Ei mean, how kin ye no-ne telly me? Ei shoulddy know ef en-bod shoulcdy. Ei gosta know. Whuddy ye thik Eim esposed tuh do effy yer gwin?"

Darby shrugged uncertainly.

"Fucknins," she said. "Es no-ne de way. Ei mean, whud iss Ei espossed te do?"

"Ye gots aller money," said Darby.

"Ei gots no-ne money."

"Ei doan. Ei gosta no-ne mun ne-mehr. Ei leef de mun aller here. Ei run way en leefy de mun." I run away and leave the money.

"Dey take it," she said. "Ye know when ye gew dey tekky de money. Dey tekky it aller. Dey leef no-ne fer mim en dey leef no-ne fer Win. Dey tekky it aller whenny ye gew."

"Know," said Darby.

"Fuckners," she said.

They both pondered silently.

"Mebbee ye doan heffta leef," said Ketra. "Ei mean, Ei talkied tuum. Dey commy here te see mim yes-tiddy. Dey sid Ei heffta telly ye tuh mekky de deal wid em. Dey assed effy ye bin here an Ei tole em ye no-ne bin here. Ei tole em ye nevne-ne bin here afore. Dey assed effy Ei gots de way te gew see ye an Ei tole em Ei coulddie gew see ye de same as dey coulddie gew see ye. Ei tole em Ei gots no-ne espessy way. Ei tole em Ei doan nevne see ye ne mehr. Dey sid effy Ei see ye te telly ye te givie selb uppy

117

en mek de deal wid em. Ei tole em Ei wouldno-ne see ye cause Ei nevne see ye ne-mehr. Like ye fergetty Ei liv. Dey sid jus in case Ei see ye tuh telly ye tuh mek de deal wid em. An Ei tole em Ei wud."

"Tolie ye who?" quizzed Darby. Who did you tell?

"Ei tole de guy who commy here."

"Here?"

"Yee. De guy. Ee commy here. Tuh see mim. Ev-bod know Ei wassy yer wif."

"Who?"

"De ol guy. De squire. Lerch."

"Squire Jammilee Lerch?" Darby asked.

"Yee. Ee es de one. Ee commy here. Ee commy here yestiddy. Lerch ee de good guy. Lerch de real good guy. Ee commy here te see mim. Ee sid ee wansted te talkie te mim. Owny te mim. Course, ee talkied owny bout ye. Ee sid how ye were fightnin ginst de sponsors, but ee sid et woanne be bad fer ye. Et woanne be bad if ye cewp'rate. Ee sid Ei should telly ye dat an ee sid Ei shoulddy be sher tuh call im on de vid es soon es Ei see ye. Ei tole im Ei woanne ne see ye. Ei tole im ye no-ne come here an Ei doan thik dey thik ye a-commy here eithner. Cause dey gots aller yer records a-reddy. Dey know ye nevne no-ne commy here. Dey know et was bad whenny we split. Dey know aller dat a-reddy cause datiss why dey tek way Win. Datiss why dey tek way Win an puddy Win in de govnenet scewel. Dey know. But jus tuh mek shir dey no commy here gin, Ei tole de Squire Ei hate ye an Ei tole em iffy ye come here Eidda killy ye owny fer mim."

"De Squire come here," repeated Darby.

"Yee, yee, ee commy richt here. But ee woan commy gin cause Ei tole im Ei hate ye an Ei tole im Ei nevne see ye enway."

Still Darby glanced around Ketra's front room suspicious-
ly.

"Ye doan haffta worry, Ei tole ye. Ei doan let no spyin. Ei
doan hef ne vid. Ei gots owny de one vid, an dats way in de back.
Noan kin hear, evne ef dey gots de override on mim. Dey kin
gew fuckky der selfs if dey try de spyin here. Der iss no-ne way
dey kin see we. No way tall. An Ei doan thik dey evne lookin, lik
Ei sid. Dey commy here jus fer precaution. Jus in case Ei mie see
ye er mebbee if Ei mai cide tuh contact ye onny me own. An Ei
woan tell em Ei see ye. Ye know Ei nevne bin dat way. Dey kin
go fuckky der selves. But Ei doan git why ye doan gew see em
yerself. How yer gonsta git way? Ye canno-ne gew ne place dey
woan find ye. Ne place en-where. An dat squire, Lerch, de good
one, ee sid Ei should tell ye ev-thin iss kay. So Ei doan git why
ye doan gew see em. How ye gonsta git way en-way?"

Darby was silent.

"How ye thik ye kin evne git way frum em?"

"Friends," he said.

"Friends who?" she shot back. "Yee, shure, ye got friends.
But who kin keep ye when dey come fer de takin? Ye got no
friends dat-ill come up ginst em. No-bod gots dem friends."

"Friends," repeated Darby.

"Whir dey gonsta puddy ye?"

"Dey tole mim te no-ne te tell whir te ye."

"Yer fucknin stoopnid," she said. "Es no-ne place ye kin
gew. Ye should gew tuh see de squire. Ee sid ee kin help ye. Ee
tole mim te telly ye if ye gew to see im yewl be kay."

"Dey strip me," said Darby.

"De Squire dint say nothin bout de strippin."

"Dey strip me."

"Yee, so, whud ye care? Whud ye care bout et en-way? Ye

woanno-ne play en-more. Deres nuddin now ye kin do wid de skin ad en-way."

"Dey strip me," repeated Darby.

"Der jus fucknin tattoos. Ye gots still yer skin."

"Gots nudth."

"Neath."

"Nudth."

"Yer Gab Darby."

"Nudth."

"Yer lots."

"Whud?"

Ketra paused. "Bud ye livvy here. Ye nevne binny ne-place bud here. An ye allerways knewd es could hap. Ye knewd aller de rules. Ye made aller de deals yerself. Whir kin ye gew? Whir else kin ye lif? Here iss whir ye allerways bin. Whir else kin ye gew? Here iss yer home."

Home. Darby recalled how, early every morning in the urb, he strolled alone on the sidewalks, mostly just to sample the air. He inhaled night's lingering odor while it still freshened the streets. He absorbed the clear, new light as the ascending sun cut obliquely against him. He passed the slumbering businesses still closed and gated—the Gap with its posters of nubiles, MacLand with its sodden aroma, the neon-glaring K-Wal outlet, Greenland with its urn filled with pills as colorful as candy. He passed all of the shops, stands, boths, food stops and offices with barely a glance. He stopped every morning at the Bit O' Caf, where, with his ads oiled and shining, he stepped to the counter to buy a tall jaf. Sipping idly at a table vid, he screened through the morning news pictures. He liked the sports segment. He skipped the clips that showed his own game-day achievements. He watched those at home.

"Iffy ye doan go wid de Squire, whud else kin ye do?" repeated Ketra. "Et woan be te bad. De Squire tole me et woan be te bad fer ye. Ee promnised. Ee sid iffy Ei got ye tuh gew wid im, Ei wouldne-nee heffta feel bad bout et, cause dey wouldno-ne do en-thin te bad tuh yuh."

"Ei beat em up," explained Darby.

"Ye beat who up?"

"Squire Jammilee Lerch."

"Ye beat em up? De Squire? Whyfer? Whud ee do? Ees so liddle. Ees olt. Deres no-ne resnon fer ye te no-ne beat up de Squire."

"Es woat Squire Lerch," he explained. "Dint touch. Bud Neighbors. One, two Neighbors commy te tek mim wid Squire de Jammilee Lerch. Ei beat em up."

"Ye beat up de Neighbors!"

"Yee."

"When?"

"Two, three days go."

"No ye dint."

"Yee."

"Two days go?"

"Yee."

"De Squire dint telly me. Ee sid ev-thin woulddy be kay fer ye. Ee dint say ye beat up on de Neighbors. Yer bucked. Whud ye yuh do et fer? Telly mim dat. Telly mim jus dat. Tally mim whud ye dewed it fer?"

"Dey commie te tek."

"Bud ye knowd deyd uh come. Ye allerways knewd de rules."

"Dey come. Dey smile. Dey mek mim ne chance."

"Yer fucknid now. Now ye got no-ne chance tall. Whud ye

gonsta do now?"

"Gwin way."

"Ye aready tole mim. Bud whir ye gwin te gew?"

"Dey tole mim no-ne te telly whir te ye."

"Bud ye gosta telly mim. Doan ye thik Ei neest te know? Whud kin Ei do when yer way? Who em Ei spowst te be when yer way?"

"Dey tole mim te no-ne te tell whir te ye."

"Bud ye knowd Ei woan-ne tell ne-bod. Ye knowd Ei doan telly em ne-thin. Ei nevne tole em en-thin afore. Ye knowe et. Dey kin all go fuckky selves. Bud Ei neest te know meself."

"Fer whud?"

"Fer whud if Ei evne neest te telly ye sumpin?"

"Telly mim whud?

"Jus sumptin."

"Nefer tole afore."

"Bud mebbee when yer way. Mebbee Ei neest te telly ye sumpin whenny yer way. Yuhl hef noan else. Lik de show days. Member de show days at de scewel. Whenny yer way ye woan-ne gew te de show days te see de Win. Ye woan see nuthnin bout ne Win. Noan else alife kin tellie ye bout de Win."

Darby considered.

"An ye knost Ei nevne-ill telly de fuckners," repeated Ketra. "Ye knost dey-ill nefer hear ne-thin from-ne mim."

"Dey tole mim no-ne te telly whir te ye."

"Bud ye hefte telly whir te mim."

"Ye see whir aller de time. Aller de time now. On vid."

"Bud ye allerways on de vid."

"Nee. No-ne mim."

"Ye mean Ei see de place whir on de vid?"

"Yee, yee. Aller de time."

"Now?"

"Yee."

Ketra rose and pounded into the hallway. She shot back at Darby, "ye doan move," just as she cut inside the first doorway she reached. Yet Darby followed her anyway, wanting simply to stay close to her. He entered her bedroom, sparsely furnished and scarcely adorned. Ketra sat on the edge of her bed, staring at an old-style television that showed the talking face of Ned Instead. Darby eased himself next to her. She did not protest. The walls of the room were barren except for a large, next-to-lifesize poster of Darby himself at play, taped up at its four corners. Next to her bed, on a nightstand that held a plain clock, Darby saw a framed photograph of Win, their son. Next to it, in another frame, stood a glamour shot of Ketra, smiling wide and revealing a deep, ample dive between her breasts.

The eager voice of Instead pierced through the silence. ". . . the aerial clips that President Jeannie promised to show to us," it said. "In just a moment you'll see actual aerial vid clips taken during a fighter strike on a building that has been identified as the Bortinca Ministry of Interior Security. This is an actual clip made by the fighter that fired the missile. Joining us now live from Central Command in Bortinca is General Handscome. Is that right, General Handscome?"

"Yes, Ned," began a second voice.

"Ye gwin dere?" Ketra asked Darby.

"Yee," he replied.

"Ye gwin te Bortinc?"

"Yee."

"Bud ye doan belonk dere."

"No-ne place else."

"Whud kin ye do dere?"

"Doan knows," said Darby.

"Es too far way."

"Yee," he agreed.

"Kin ye lif wid de borons?"

"Dey say."

"An whud bout mim? Ei gots nutnin whin yer gwin."

"Gots nutnin now."

"Ei woan be de sluggers once-wif ne-mehr."

Darby looked down at his colored chest and arms.

"Dey strip me," he said.

". . . now held by rebels," chirped the voice of General Handscome. " . . . important target . . . ."

"Ei hoped ye coulddy least mek a deal wid em."

"No-ne de deal. Dey strip me."

"Den whud ye evne commy here fer?" Ketra asked quietly.

"Commy te see ye."

"Why te see mim?" she asked. "Ye dint commy te see mim evnerny oth chance ye gots."

"Commy so you kin remember me."

"Member ye?"

"Yee."

"Course Ei member ye. Ye Gadubby de Slugger. Ev-bod member ye."

"Ne-bod knowst me."

"Ev-bod knowst ye. Ev-bod seest ye ev-day on de vid. Ev-bod member dat."

"They doan know. It's just de vid. It's just a vid picture. They don't know Gab Darby. You know Gab Darby. Ei wanny you to remember me."

"Ei allerways member ye."

"And Win."

"Win allerways member ye."

"Woan see Win ne-mehr."

"Nee, nee, ye woan see im ne-mehr at de fence at de scew-el."

"Nee."

"Win tole me ye commy der te see im et-times."

"Woan commy ne-mehr."

"Dey-ll tek ye fer sure at de scewel."

"Gwin way."

"Yee, yee, ye gwin way."

"Ye tell im?"

"Tell im whud?"

"Tell im why Ei gwin."

"He-ill knowst a-ready. He-ill see ev-thin aller on de vid. Ei bet Win seest it a-ready."

"Kin ye git im?"

"Git im?"

"Git im home."

"Take im from de scewel?"

"Yee, yee, take im from de scewel."

"Nee, nee, dey nevne lest im outter de scewel now. Efter ye gwin he-ill hefta stay in dere allerways."

"Ye see im?"

"Course Ei-ill see im. Yee. Yee. Ei woan stop-ne seein im fer notnin. Ei doan care whud de fuckers mebbee sayst te mim."

"Tell im?"

"Tell im whud?"

"Ei luf."

"Dey-ill talk rel bad bout ye now."

"Tell im Ei luf."

"Ei tell im et fer sure."

"Luf you, too."

"Nee, nee, ets fucknin bushit. Ye doan luffy mim."

"Yee."

"Nee. Nee, ye doan."

"Yee."

"Nee, nee, ye doan luffy mim. Ye doan. Ye canno-ne telly mim now. Now es yer gwin way. Whud kin Ei spost te do now when yer gwin?"

"Member mim."

She sat silently. The voice of Instead droned in the background: "General Handscome, the new commander of our Bortinca Peace-keeping troops, will be back with us a little later."

Darby rose laboriously from the bed.

"When he returns," went Instead, "the general will have the aerial vids we've been telling you about. He'll show us our successful attack on the Bortinca Ministry of Interior Security, a very important target."

The small clock on the stand beside Ketra's bed showed Darby's hour was ending. He understood that Paleo would not wait if Darby arrived late at the drive through below them.

In the living room he bent laboriously to pick up the shirt that concealed his body. As he put on the garment she told him, "Ei allerways sid de skin ad woudst git yer kilt." During their marriage Darby had simply ignored her vague superstitions. He had smirked at her unfounded intuitions. He had mocked her preternatural distrust of officialdom and its consumptive largesse.

As slowly as his time would allow, Darby picked up the jacket and slipped his arms inside its sleeves. He buttoned up its front. He hoisted the vacuumer onto his back and with sad care he cinched the straps on his shoulders. He turned to face Ketra.

"Yer no-nee ne boron," she said to him.

"Knowst," he replied.

"When ye gwin way?"

"Gwin way righ now."

"Ei whoan-ne tell em whir ye gwin."

"Knowst," said Darby.

"Ei whoan-ne tell te ne-bod."

"Tell te Win," he said.

"Nee, nee, Ei woan tell-ne te Win. Winnie too liddle. Ee migh tell some-bod."

"Tell im Ei luf."

"Yee. Course. Ei tell im de slugger luf de Win."

"Luf you."

"Doan tellie mim."

"Luf you."

"Puddy ye onst de hat. Ye doan-ne fergit de hat."

Darby snugged it over his crown and swiped down the brim to conceal his face. He looked at her a last time. Ketra plodded across the room to him and wrapped him in a pinching embrace. She could not close her arms around his bulk and her hands fumbled awkwardly against the machine on his back. Darby wrapped her entirely within him.

"Ei luf," he repeated.

"Ei luf," she responded.

As Darby reached for the door he saw tears pool deeply in her eyes. He left her. His own face pinched and puckered from an upwell of tears as he walked through the dim hallway. He tugged the brim lower, feeling suddenly grateful to be wearing the garish hat.

## CHAPTER ELEVEN

"But why do they keep following me wherever I go?" complained Jantillus Flavin. "Every place I go, every time I turn around, more American soldiers are after me and I have to run away again. Why are they chasing *me*? I didn't start this. I didn't start any of it. And I'm not the one who's fighting against them now. If they really want to stop this they should go after some of those other officers. They should go after the ones who chased out Bortus and who chased out all of his goons. They're the new generals now. They're the ones who started all of this fighting. They're the ones with all the soldiers behind them. The Americans should go after them and arrest them and arrest all their soldiers. That's the way they would end this whole thing once and for all."

"But you have soldiers behind you too," said Captain Actus.

"But it's not the same," countered Flavin.

"And there's more and more soldiers coming here every

day to join up with you," Captain Actus went on. He was small, quick, and clever, with hands that turned finely around the emphasis of an idea. His friend, Jantillus Flavin, slouched from weariness as he listened. "The soldiers are running away from all the other generals and they're coming here to join up with you," said Actus. "They want to fight under you. They don't trusts those others. They think all those other generals, they just want to get the power for themselves. That's why they went after Bortus: to take the power for themselves. But even their own soldiers don't trust them now. After all, they were all friends of Bortus's once or maybe they were friends of Bortus's generals. That's how they got to be officers in the first place. But nobody likes them. Nobody trusts them. Sure, their soldiers were happy enough to take over the palace for them and to take over all of the compounds. But that was just to get rid of the crooks. Now that they're gone, they don't want other crooks to take over. That would be just as bad. That's why they want you. They trust you. Why else do you think all the soldiers are coming here? Why else do you think they're all getting behind you?"

"But the American soldiers started chasing me before I had this whole Bortono army around me," replied Flavin. "That's why the Bortos are coming here: they're coming here because the Americans are coming here. And the Americans are here because I'm here. And that's the part I don't understand. They start out trying to arrest me. But the more they try to arrest me, the more the Bortonos come around to protect me. Now I have a whole army of American soldiers trying to arrest me and a whole army of Bortono soldiers trying to protect me and I don't even know why they want to arrest me in the first place."

"But you are the general," insisted Captain Actus. "We made you the general."

"But I don't know anything about how to be a general."

"But they trust you. They want to follow you."

"I don't want anybody to follow me. I want them all to go home. I want to go home myself. That's what I was trying to do when this whole thing started. I left the army to go home like everybody else. Then the Americans started chasing me."

"They chased you because they know you are our leader."

"But I am not your leader. I was never your leader. Not the kind of leader you mean. I think they're after the wrong guy. They keep saying they want this person named Vestin. That's what we keep hearing on the news reports and everything: someone named Vestin is behind all the fighting and the Americans are going to get him. I don't know anyone named Vestin and no one I talk to has ever known anyone named anything like Vestin. No one's ever even heard of him. I think that would be a woman's name anyway, wouldn't it? Vestin? But this Vestin is supposed to be a man and he's supposed to be a great national leader. I've never been a national leader. Not like that."

"Now some of our own soldiers call you Vestin."

"But isn't it a woman's name?"

"I don't know. It's just a nickname. Don't think of it like that."

"But what am I supposed to do? I'm not Vestin, no matter what anybody calls me. And you, you can elect me. You can call me your general and that's all very easy to do. But I don't know how to be a general. I never learned that."

"But you had all the same training as the rest of us. At the same schools and everything. And you were even at the troubles down in Ramtuk. You distinguished yourself."

"But I was never a general. And those were just little battles down at Ramtuk. This time they've gone and started a whole war. I don't know how to fight a war."

"But there is no one else."

"But there has to be somebody better than me. I don't know what to do. I don't know how to fight a war."

Colonel Altan, a stark, serious man who had remained in the shadows at the edge of the room, stepped up. "You attack," he asserted. "You fight a war by attacking." He sounded impatient. He had watched too long from the margin, where he and all of the other officers had agreed to remain while Captain Actus endeavored to persuade Jantillus Flavin. Actus knew Flavin better than any of the other officers in the room. Actus, they had figured, could haggle with the reluctant general as an old-time chum, because Captain Actus had grown up with Jantillus Flavin. They had been playmates in the same little burg. They had attended the same schools and they had kissed and trysted some of the same budding girls. But Captain Actus might plod too long making irrelevant counterpoints. Or so feared Colonel Altan, who recognized that the present opportunity for battle would soon escape them. Therefore he repeated his assertion: "In a war you attack."

"I know you attack," replied Flavin. "I have always understood the precepts. But it is when to attack and where to attack and even how to attack. Those are the questions. Those are the specifics one needs to consider. It is the specifics, after all, and not the general precepts, that will make you successful."

Captain Actus smiled inwardly. Silently he yielded to the intrusion by Colonel Altan, who was bold enough to challenge Flavin. Actus had seen Jantillus Flavin rise when challenged before.

"But knowing the precepts is the most important first step," argued the colonel. "If you understand that you must attack, then figuring out the specifics takes only some care and attention. If you understand the precepts, and you have the support and the loyalty of your soldiers on top of the precepts, then you are a great leader. It doesn't matter what you say about yourself."

"No," said Flavin. "You can only be a great leader after you have led. Only after you have accomplished something. After you have proven yourself. I have not proven anything. I have not done anything. It's just the Americans and their President Jeannie who are making this whole thing up. They want this Vestin. Okay, let them take Vestin. Who would miss her? But I am not Vestin. But they chase me like I am. And then all the soldiers, they also get this idea that I am the leader here. I am not the leader. And in fact, it is the support and the loyalty of all these men that bothers me so much. Why should they put so much faith in me? They don't know me. They only hear all the American talk about some fearless Vestin who nobody knows and somehow it gets assumed that this Vestin is me."

"But you've always had a very big reputation, Janto," said Captain Actus. "People liked you and trusted you long before any of this."

"But never for anything like this before," Flavin replied. "I've never fought a whole war before. I don't know how to fight a war."

"You attack," repeated Colonel Altan.

"Yes, I know you attack. But again, the question is when to attack. And where to attack."

"Look," insisted Altan. "Look at the weather out there. This will keep up for days. We know that for sure. We know how it storms in this season. It will keep up for one more day at least. When the storm is this heavy, they don't see so good with their eye in the sky. Therefore the *when* to attack is now, when they can't see us moving. And if we attack right now, well then, the only place we can attack them is right here."

"All the soldiers are all very well prepared right now," contributed Captain Actus.

"But we would have to cross the river to attack them," said Flavin. "Even if they can't see us from the sky, here on the ground they will see us when we try to cross the river. Of course, we could always cross it at night. That would help. But I still think their lookouts and their sentries would see us. Even at night. Probably even in this storm."

"I don't think they would see us tonight," Colonel Altan retorted. "Today is their big holiday. Remember? Today is Labor Day. They never work on Labor Day. The soldiers have it in their union contract. It's a holiday. Skeleton staff. They don't do anything today. Everybody takes it off. Ever the officers take it off, and they're not even in the union. They spend the whole day with the camp girls. That's why none of the ladies are here today. They make more money on the other side. With the officers. The soldiers just stay all day in their camp or their barracks or wherever. The union bosses come and make speeches to them. Then they have their cookouts and they drink beer. Everybody drinks beer. It's a holiday. The men and the women go off together. Sure, they'll put some sentries out, but I don't think they'll see us if we move today and cross the river after it gets dark."

"Yes, of course, I know all about Labor Day," said Flavin. "But we still have to get across safely and get in a good position to attack."

"Look here," said the colonel. He stepped up to the folding table that held the map that Captain Actus had uncurled at the start of his conversation with Flavin. Colonel Altan opened it further, by spreading the two black rifles that held down the map's curled edges

"This is where they have the most soldiers," Colonel Altan pointed. "In this little town here. Three regiments. That's too many for us to fight all at once. But it would take them at least a day to get to where we are here, and that's after they got everything ready to move, which could take them another whole day at least. But here, right here on the river, here in Belnish they have a whole other regiment. We're practically right on top of Belnish right now. We can cross the river at this spot right here and be on top of them, be right in Belnish, before they even know what hits them."

"No," said Flavin. "That's not a good place. It's too open. I know this country. They might see us come across there even in this storm. Even on Labor Day. And even if they didn't see us then, look at this area here. This is where we would end up. It's too flat. We'd have this flat, open plain to cross. There's no cover here. It's all farms. And they have the hills up here. No, I think the best place to cross is here, further up north. I know this river. We could get across here. You have to remember that on a night like tonight, with this storm and the wind and everything, just getting across the river is going to be hard. You have to think about that. But we could get across here. The current is better. And see, the banks here make it easier for crossing if we cross up here. It's further away, I know. But we could make it across the river a lot more easily and there's no way they would ever see us if we crossed up here. Then we would have to march down to Belnish, of course, but it's not too far away. Maybe ten miles. I bet it's not even ten miles. I'd say it's only nine miles. We'd have enough time to cross the river and still get to Belnish for a surprise attack. We'd get there by dawn. And look at the cover we'd have when we're marching down from here. And we'd have a good position to attack from, too. The only problem is getting across the river in the first place."

"But there are lots of boats," said Colonel Altan. "We have been collecting boats wherever we can all up and down the river. Captain Weltic, can you tell us how many boats we have so far?"

"I don't know the count exactly," spoke young Captain Weltic as he stepped out of the shadow. "They are all different sizes anyway, because we are taking whatever people can give us. So the number doesn't matter so much. The question is how many men can we carry across at a time. For that I can tell you that we would have to make at least three trips back and forth across the river. Maybe four. It depends on how many soldiers you want to get across."

"And what about down here," asked Flavin. He poked his finger at a spot on the map that showed the river bend away just south of Belnish. "Do you also have boats ready to cross more men down here?"

The captain shot a glance of uncertainty at Colonel Altan, his commander. That question had not come up in their earlier planning. He was sure it had not come up, but now he wondered if he had done something wrong by neglecting to collect boats in the south.

"But why would we need boats down there," protested Colonel Altan.

"I do have some boats down there," said the young captain cautiously. "Not too many. But some. They're just waiting down there, because we haven't been able to bring them up yet. You have to be careful how you bring them up past Belnish. With the Americans in the town you can't just motor past with a whole bunch of boats. Everything has to look normal. So we left some down there."

"How many," demanded Flavin.

Again Captain Weltic shot an uncertain glance at Colonel Altan. "I don't know how many," he replied. "Not too many. They're just the ones we couldn't get up."

"But why do we need boats down there anyway," protested Colonel Altan once again.

"The precepts," Flavin replied. "Remember the precepts, Colonel Altan. To attack. Yes. To win. Yes. But then what do you do, colonel? I'll tell you what. You press your advantage. To drive the American's out of Belnish would be a very great thing. But then what are we supposed to do, stand there and wave them goodbye? Look at this here." Flavin pushed his finger emphatically onto a spot on the map. "If we come down from here to attack, the Americans will have to leave the town this way, to the south. There will be no other way for them to go. Therefore, if we also cross the river down here, we can be waiting for them. We can meet them when they're in retreat. We attack them again here when they're retreating. We can use a smaller force after they leave the town. Then our victory is complete, Colonel Altan."

The colonel stood nodding his head in comprehension.

"We could cross in these two places down here," Flavin went on. "Three companies cross here, and two companies right here. Then they would wait. When the Americans retreated down from Belnish, then our companies would join up like this and we'd have them."

"So we cross in three places," said the colonel.

"Three places," confirmed General Flavin. "We cross up here, and then we march down nine miles for the main attack.

At the same time we cross down here, and also down here, so we can block their retreat."

"Can we do that?" Colonel Altan asked the hesitant Captain Weltic.

"Well, yes, but, we might need more boats," the captain replied.

"Then you'd better go to start getting them right away," said Flavin to the young officer. "Of course," he went on, "we would also need to start moving our soldiers toward the river right away. It would take them a while just to get across in the night."

"Then we need to know who will cross where," said Colonel Altan. "We need to know who will command the main attack from the north, and who will command the second attack down here."

Captain Actus broke in, "I would vote that you take your companies down here for the southern attack, Colonel Altan. Your soldiers are trained better than some of these others. They've been together longer. They'll be able to stay together better down here even though there's not as many of them."

"But we need good soldiers up here too, for the main attack," Altan put in.

"Yes, but there will be more of them up here for the main attack," Captain Actus responded. "Up here they'll have more safety in numbers, as they say. What we'll need here for the main attack is a good leader that the men will all obey and follow."

"Yes, that's very important," the colonel agreed. "We'll need more companies for this main attack. We'll have to lump together companies that haven't been together before. There will be a lot of men here who don't know each other. They haven't been together too long. They haven't trained together. And they will have to push their attack very vigorously to keep the surprise. They will have to trust in their commander."

"You're the only one who can lead them, Janto," said Captain Actus to his childhood friend.

As he stared at the map, Jantillus Flavin silently nodded his head.

# CHAPTER TWELVE

When President Jeannie Welk-Emerson-Landose saw the cue that meant that the studio eye that faced her blankly was now preparing to beam her video speech, she pulled in her bottom lip. Carefully, concealing the lip inside her closed mouth, she held it pinched between her teeth, affecting an expression of grave determination that might also be taken for anger. When the little red light flashed on, showing that the eye was now finally broadcasting, she held the bit-lip pose, pausing appropriately before beginning to speak, allowing her resolute expression some time to seep into the psyches of the millions and millions of people who now saw her face well framed upon their vids. First Adviser Mel Santee had commandeered an all-channel appearance for this evening. Vid watchers could not switch to another view to avoid this prime-time speech by President Jeannie. She waited longer, her lip held affectedly, until she saw the subtle nod from Santee, who sat just to the side of the glowering studio eye. She began her script.

"Good prime-time to all of you. Thank you for viewing and let me give you my promise that I won't take too long," she said before her next pause.

"I have visited you here many times before to talk about the brave action of our army. And I have told you many times before how we have the best army in the world. And I want you to know that we still do. Without a doubt.

"But by now you might have already heard about the sneak attack against our army in Bortinca. I'm here to tell you that it's true: nearly a thousand of our brave soldiers were captured and taken prisoner. And some were even killed. But we don't know how many yet, because we're still negotiating to get our brave soldiers returned and so we haven't been able to add them all up yet. But we could not wait for me to come here to tell this very important message to everybody at once. Before you hear other reports that won't be true, I'm here to tell you the true report of what happened, and to tell you exactly what I'm doing to get back for this sneak attack by the Bortonese rebels under their leader, Vestin.

"First, I'm sorry to have to tell you that it's true that the Bortonese rebels crossed a river call the Narfink River last night and made a surprise attack very early this morning that surprised our brave soldiers.

"There's two things that make me very mad about this attack," she said. As she spoke, President Jeannie pinched together her thumb and her foremost two fingers, forming a parrot-beak shape that she used with deliberate effect by holding it chest-level and striking with it, nodding it upward and downward and upward and downward to emphasize her words. "The first thing that makes me mad is that the weather is very rainy and stormy in Bortinca right now, especially around the little town where they attacked our brave soldiers. The weather is so bad that we couldn't pick them up with the air tracking that we use all the time to protect our brave soldiers and keep them out of harm's way. We couldn't see that they were lining up for a surprise attack and it makes me real mad that Vestin would use the weather unfairly like that.

"The other thing that makes me mad is that they did it when our soldiers just finished their celebration of the Important Day of Labor Day. Labor Day was yesterday and the only way Vestin and his rebels could have attacked so early today was by crossing the river and making all their movements to get into position when it was still Labor Day. That's the only way they even could have surprised and captured so many of our brave soldiers: by sneaking around on the Important Day of Labor Day."

President Jeannie paused, turning in her bottom lip once again, holding it inside her straight, serious mouth and maintaining the pose for emphasis. Upon the silent cue from Santee she began again.

"Labor Day is an Important Day that I think is very important. I'm real mad that Vestin would violate this real important day and I think that shows what he's made of.

"I want you all to know how bad I feel for our brave soldiers. I feel real bad for our children, too. I do not want the children of our great country to grow up believing that Vestin or anyone else can beat us with his tricks and his lying like that. Our brave soldiers were very brave in this battle. Vestin tried to send even more of his rebels across the Narfink River but we stopped them before they even got across. We stopped two whole armies from getting across. But this one rebel army that made it across was led personally by Vestin. They were able to trick us by moving on Labor Day. That's the only way Vestin was able to capture so many of our brave soldiers.

"But I will not let the children of our great country grow up thinking that anyone can do that to us. That's why I gave the order to General Handscome today to start terrible ground attacks to bring all the rebels to justice.

"It's time to win this war once and for all," the President intoned. "We have the best army in the world. So now we're going to attack Vestin's army and destroy it on the ground. I talked about this with all my advisers. General Handscome and all his brave pilots have already done a very good job of destroying all the important buildings and all the other places like that down in Bortinca. And I want to take this time to say thank you to all the smart people in all the agencies and the groups that approved our successful, Urban Air Strike Program. Thanks to them our brave pilots were able to blow up their headquarters and their Ministry of Internal Security and their Ministry of External Relations and their vid center and all their communications outposts and everything like that. We blew up all the buildings that Vestin had taken over for the execution of his war against our brave soldiers. We showed you the vid clips of a lot of those big attacks. We showed you the buildings right when they were being blown up. At the time, we hoped that after all his important buildings were destroyed, Vestin would be ready to negotiate with us to begin the peace process. But now we can say for sure that he doesn't care about peace. He doesn't even care about the safety of his own people. Because by destroying all his command buildings from the air, our brave pilots have already cut off his ability to wage war. But he still uses tricks to attack us, even though it puts his own soldiers in so much danger.

"Therefore General Handscome will now use his army on the ground the same way our planes in the air have crippled Vestin with our Urban Air Strike Program." Her parrot hand pecked for emphasis, nodding upward and downward and upward and downward. "I will get even for all the brave men and women of America who fought against his lying and his tricks with their last ounce of strength, until they couldn't hold out and were captured. I won't give up until every brave American soldier gets home. We have the greatest army in the world. The next time I come here to talk to you, it will be with news about our victories in the new ground war against Vestin and his rebel army."

She dropped her hand to her side.

"Thank you and good luck America."

## CHAPTER THIRTEEN

When Gab Darby woke early on only his second morning in Bortinca, he sniffed dank river air waft in the open window and immediately he realized that he should have walked farther before he had stopped for a room the night before. But in the darkness this place had seemed already far enough from the water. And after the sagging, sooty woman had led him among so many dim, snaking corridors to this small chamber far in the back of the building, Darby had welcomed the window. He had not realized that the spongy, equatorial air would carry the brackish scent so far. He had spent his first, fitful night of exile sleeping on cartons inside a stifling, steel-walled warehouse that stood at the river siding. He would return there this morning to work. He had wanted to escape the water at least for the night.

He closed the window before fumbling to find his clothing in the faint light that leaked under his door. Outside the door the lamp shined so dimly that Darby started through the low hallway before his eyes accommodated the change. He made his way through the labyrinth to the food counter at the front end of the tenement. He found the same smeared, soiled woman standing idly at the grille. She had told him last night that breakfast was included in the fee for the room. She served him buttered eggs.

Outside Darby whiffed the sodden air once more. He started down the low-sloping hill, following the roadway that was chocked by a teeming jumble of low houses and huts and even some shops that served simple utility: a laundry stop, a poultry shed, an electrical parts store. He passed a ramshackle stand that dispensed beer in thin plastic cups. Two men sat beside it, sipping disinterestedly, squatting so low they seemed almost to cower on the plastic crates strewn carelessly on the pavement. They watched Darby as he passed.

When Darby turned a hard left the river dropped broadly into his view. Descending nearer, he passed the Caterpillar factory that had gone to weeds when so many of its welders, its torch men, its saw wielders and metal bangers ran off to join the Borto army. Unable to make more dozers and loaders, its owners had abandoned the sprawling plant. Farther on, he passed the small cigarette works, which kept operating not only because it required few workers. Eager and generous buyers also demanded its products. For the cigarette maker, the only problem posed by the war was to find ways to reach its customers up in America. The railroad no longer moved reliably. Trucks were usually searched, and their trailer-loads of cigarettes were too often hijacked by soldiers from one side or another. Because of the shipping embargo, big cargo boats no longer tied up at the long dock where the river road ended. Therefore the cigarette makers had learned to rely on little pleasure craft that smuggled out crates without raising suspicions. Workers shuttled down pallet-loads of packaged cigarettes to a long, low, flat-roofed shed that sided the river wharf. Darby had been hired the day before, his first full day in the country, to fill the berths and cabins of the little boats with the brown boxes packed with cigarettes.

The man who had hired Darby—whom Darby had found with two other men inside the shed, all of them sitting idly in a walled-off nook where an air conditioner rattled ferociously in the flimsy wall—had given him just one instruction: load the little boats quickly, because the pilots felt anxious to push off without lingering. Therefore Darby hefted the boxes three at a time from the stifling little shed. The first boat that arrived that morning took only five. It came with only a pilot. Next came a larger craft, with a pilot and a sharp-eyed teen who did all the deck scrambling. After the teen tied up the boat, Darby pushed boxes into every corner below the deck, stooping and hunching inside the cramped cabin. The pilot, meanwhile, disappeared inside the shed, presumably to transact with the boss who sat in the chilled small nook. When he returned, the pilot stood idly on the wharf, smoking. The teen stood beside him, smoking. They watched Darby shuffle boxes from the shed. They watched him bow and stoop to hide the boxes inside the cabin.

The routine repeated monotonously. By the time he had loaded a handful of the pleasure boats, the sun stood high. The concrete wharf sintered beneath it. The concealing shirt made by Antrina, soaked now with his sweat, clung awkwardly to Darby. He took it off. The boatmen who arrived now grew imperious. They sneered at him. They mocked him with needless orders: *hey, don't put it there; I need room to move around down there you know. Don't throw those so hard; you know, my people won't take the ones you break. I have to get out of here soon, you know; I don't like you taking your time when the eyes are watching.* In the mid afternoon Darby covered himself with the shirt again. He loaded the small boats in silence.

# CHAPTER FOURTEEN

When the camp girls stopped coming, the soldiers who had gone up to the high hideout with Bortus began to wonder about the American garrison nearby. On the second day with no girls, a sergeant took two soldiers down the high ridge and around the steep roundel to the neighboring encampment. The three men returned in barely an hour. The sergeant reported at once to the lieutenant in charge of the loyal guards who had escorted Bortus to the mountain retreat. He told the lieutenant that he did not bring back any girls because, apparently, the girls had left the camp after the Americans abandoned it. The Americans had been gone for two or three days, he estimated. They had stripped the place, which led the sergeant to conclude that they did not plan to return.

This discovery brought grave concern to the guards in the mountain compound. They numbered only about two dozen. That had been enough to protect Bortus and General Frin from ambush or assault on the night they had fled the urban compound. But the loyal protectors knew that they could not withstand any kind of determined attack up here without the help of the American garrison that used to be nearby.

The lieutenant went immediately to report the desertion to Bortus and General Frin. When he could not raise a response from the inner compound where the leaders hid themselves, the lieutenant called three soldiers to break into the building. They discovered that Bortus and Frin had fled in the night, escorted by the few defenders that Frin always kept close to him.

The two dozen men gathered in the plush inner compound to deliberate. But they drank up so much of the liquor that Bortus kept stashed in a closet that they fell fast asleep before they approached a decision.

Patters and sprays of gunfire woke them in the morning. The shooting stopped after a moment and when the loyal protectors peered warily outside the compound, they saw that rebel soldiers had shot up the mammoth statue of Bortus that stood just outside the main gate. The attackers stood out in the open. A few paced leisurely around the statue, gazing up at it, self-assured, unconcerned about any activity inside the closed gate.

The protectors' lieutenant led out his men behind a white flag. He approached an indifferent captain who appeared to be the rebels' ranking officer. After he saluted, the lieutenant reported that Bortus and General Frin were no longer inside. They had fled only the night before, he reported. The captain replied coolly that he had already figured that out. The lieutenant asked the captain if these men around the statue represented the captain's full force. The captain replied indifferently that they did. The lieutenant considered for a moment. There appeared to be only about a dozen of them.

Two of the rebel soldiers leaned their weight hard against the statue's legs, pushing hard with their hands to try to topple it. Their captain watched them indifferently. The lieutenant informed the captain that a loader was parked inside the compound. He said that he didn't think the captain's men could pull down so large a statue, but that the loader with a cable attached could drag it to the ground very easily. After a moment the lieutenant repeated that he could send in a man to get the loader. The captain replied that the lieutenant could bring out the loader if he wanted or he could leave it inside if he wanted.

After the big statue was spilled, the lieutenant told the captain that he believed that General Frin and Bortus had fled deeper into the mountains. The lieutenant asked the captain if he and his two-dozen protectors could join up with him. He said that since Bortus had only a day's head start, he was certain he could catch him. The lieutenant was certain he could lead the captain to Bortus and to Frin to dispense justice there on the spot.

The captain said the lieutenant could go fuck himself. The captain said he knew these mountains well enough, and that he and his rangers could find Bortus unaided and do with him whatever they wanted.

The lieutenant then asked what he should do with his two-dozen men at the compound while the captain was gone. The captain replied that the lieutenant and the protectors should clear out long before the captain got back.

## CHAPTER FIFTEEN

As he trudged wearily upward on the long-sloping road, as he passed the frantic cigarette works and as he passed the silent Caterpillar plant where high weeds in the yard threatened to breech the building's stained walls, as he made the hard right turn where the river disappeared behind him and the street intermixed with shacks, shanties, shops, houses and the open beer booth where sooted men gathered night and day to drink, Darby felt grateful that his boarding house stood so close to the water's edge. He had loaded small boats for twenty-seven straight days. He had taken no breaks in between. The monotony of the labor numbed him. The singeing fury of the sun numbed him. The snubbing by the boatmen and the silent indifference of the warehouse boss who stayed always inside the air-cooled nook numbed him. Through the day vitality had seeped away from him as endlessly he stooped and lifted and climbed and stacked. Pain accumulated. He trudged. High up the road, obscured by long shadows, the low-sprawling tenement opened generously into his view.

Although he had vowed never to return to the rooming house, after his first day on the wharf Darby had gone back because he did not want to walk a step farther. He returned after that because the pot-bellied woman gave him his dinner. In the morning she gave him a second plate of buttered eggs and as he ate those she wrapped a sandwich of mash and grilled meat and packed two doughnuts in a bag for him to take for his lunch. The house let out rooms only by the night, but the woman held the same, distant chamber in the back corner for Darby. The room was the quietest in the house, because its corridor snaked so far from the noisy street. And because the woman kept the room secure for him, Darby stashed his shoulder bag there when he walked down to the river each morning. He didn't need to tote it along. She took care of Darby's washing as well, carting his sweat-soiled shirts and his rank briefs to the cleaning shop for the few coins he gave her more as a tip than a payment, meant to cover the launderer's fee and then leave some excess for her, to sop her through the long hours of idle brilliance, while she waited for boarders to stagger into the house after the sky disillumened and after even the sun grew tired of the day. He had stayed on account of the woman. But after his twenty-seventh day loading crates at the liffy, Darby appreciated the house mostly because it stood so close.

The next morning Darby woke again when the smell of river bracken infused his room. He dressed in the dark. He found the food counter in the front of the house characteristically abandoned, since the other tenants always stirred so late from their stupors. The squat, oily housekeeper had already laid thick potato slices onto the grille, sautéing them slowly for

Darby. After he settled on a stool at the counter, as the woman made ready to break eggs upon the spitting griddle, she looked over her shoulder to speak to Darby. That was something new: he was unaccustomed to hearing her talk in the morning.

"I got something to tell you today," she began. "I heard it yesterday. Yesterday at night I heard it when the men here send me to the beer stand over there to get them some beers. Some always sends me. Almost ev'ry night after they eat some sends me over there to buy beers for them and bring them back here for them to drink. I doan like to go but they send me because sometimes they don't even pay me anything for the beer. Sometimes I need to scream at them just to get the money for what the beer costs. They doan gimme any extra for walkin' over there all the time. I doan wanna go anyway. Even if they gave me extra I doan wanna go over there 'cause the men sitting there on them boxes they always say things to me when I'm gettin' the beers. Them men over there are big pigs. They always want me in beds."

She twisted her body sideways to look at Darby more squarely. He wondered if her chest jutted out intentionally. Perhaps she had thrown her breasts upward only for balance.

"That's what I need to tell you ' bout today. ' Bout what they said to me yesterday when I went over there for some beers last night. You were sleepin' then way back in your room. I went over there and some of the men on the crates sittin' down out there made fun of you. I was waitin' to get the beers and that one who's got the ugly red blotch all over his face he asked where I bin and he said he's so sad 'cause he doan git to buy me nuthin and he doan git to take me to beds no more 'cause now I'm too good for him 'cause now I got the big slugger who takes all the care of me. When he said that all the others there laughed when

157

he said that. One of 'em said you should buy me new clothes but you doan have ' nough money to buy 'em 'cause you do all that work that you doan get paid for. He laughed and all the others they laughed real hard when he said that. Doan you know they been cheatin' you? They been takin' all the extra money you make for 'em and now they're laughin' at you for not knowin' it."

She set down eggs on a plate on the counter in front of him.

"Git pay ev-dee," said Darby.

"But how much you git paid?"

"Dey pidee mim whud dey sayd."

"What they said at the start." With a quick turn of her wrist she laid fat, golden-fried potato slices onto his plate from her spatula. She salted them while she spoke. "Oh, yeah, sure," she said, "they pay you what they said at the start when they hired you for. But that's what they're laughin' at now. Now they're makin' lots more money 'cause yer doin all the work but now they're not payin' ya no more for it. They keep it all for themselves now, all the extra they git now that you bin workin' for 'em down there. Dint ya notice now that lots more boats come in? Dint ya see 'em go in every time they come to pay for yer loadin'? That's what they do it down there. The boatmen they pay for all the boxes they take and then they pay extra to the warehouse man for all his work in loadin' 'em. They can't load 'em themselfs. He doan allow it. They hafta let you load 'em for 'em 'cause that's the rule he made if they want the ciggies but now that yer loadin' lots more boats he's makin' lots more money from 'em but you doan git any of it. That's why they're laughin' at ya. Lots more boats come in now 'cause you load 'em so fast and you load 'em so good that the boatmen they feel safer to come here now. They zip in and they zip out so they come here more all the time. Now the warehouse man he's got all extra money from all the new boats and all you got for it is more work to do and all the others ' round here they laughin' at you 'cause you got no more of the new money. They like to laugh at you anyway but now they kin laugh 'cause they say yer a stupid."

She turned back to the cook top. Clinging grime dulled the sweat that banded the back of her neck.

"I think today is the day you march down there and you tell 'em they gotta give you more money. You tell 'em that right away in the morning. You tell the wareman that yer gonna quit this very day lest he gives you more money. He woan let ya go. He'll give ya more money 'cause without you he woan get all the boats any more. You tell 'em you seen all the more boats that come in every day now. You tell 'em you doan like it that yer doin all the work that's makin' all the boats come in and now yer workin' more and more 'cause of all the boats but he's keepin' all the new money. You tell him he's gotta pay more of it to you."

"Yee, yee," said Darby. "Bud whud mehr dey pidee mim?"

"You tell 'em you want more for every box you load up. Here," she said. "Here. You take this pen here with you. It's a real good pen but I doan mind if I give it to you and I find another one to use. You take this pen with you today and ev'ry box you load up you make a line with this pen on a box or maybe some paper you lay over on the side where you know it's okay. You make one line for every box of ciggies you load up and then after the day you count 'em all up. When the wareman pays you after the day you get one extra dollar for every the boxes you loaded up. You still get what they paid from the start but now you get extra too. Now you get one extra dollar extra for every box, 'cause now you load up so many boxes for 'em."

"Es lots," said Darby.

"It's lots and lots al'right but you tell 'em they been cheatin' you and now they gotta stop cheatin' or you woan load no more boats for 'em. It's for you that I'm tellin' ya to do it. It's not for me that I'm tellin' ya. It's for you. I want you to have the money that's yers. I doan want any bit of it for me. Tonight I kin come to your room. After the sun I kin come and we can beds and ev'rything and fun and you doan hafta pay me nothin' for it. You kin give me just anything you want or any little bit extra you have left over and I doan care what it is. It's whate'er you want."

Darby looked up from his plate in surprise. Her back was turned to him still as she fussed with the grille.

"Ei pidee de room ev-dee," he said.

"And you doan hafta pay me no more for yer room and you doan hafta pay me for these lunches I make ev'ry day for ya or for the suppers I make or the breakfasts I make. That's all from me for you and I never asked you for any extra money for any of it and I'm not askin' for any extra money for it now. I kin come tonight for beds and that's for you and you kin give me any extra money you want and I don't ask you for how much."

Another lodger entered the kitchen for breakfast. He was a worker like Darby. The woman reverted to her usual silent indifference as she began to make his meal. By now the sloping road outside had started to brighten with the earliest hope of the sun. Soon smuggling little pleasure craft would arrive at the liffy. Darby could not wait for the lodger to finish his meal and leave the counter for a chance to pick up the conversation again. He left the cook-room silently. He let the woman's proposition stand unanswered—if it even permitted an answer, since it sounded more like an assertion than a proposition. He began his descent to the river at a brisker pace this morning, determined to confront the loading boss before the first small vessel arrived.

But at the shed he found the small, walled-in nook abandoned. Even the frantic little air conditioner in the wall was silent. To Darby the weird stillness reinforced the housekeeper's account: the boss was cheating him, and now that Darby knew about it, the boss had stayed away this morning to avoid him.

The sputter of an approaching boat beckoned Darby outside. He would load it, he figured. He couldn't send the pilot away empty, after all. He would load every other boat that came too, and—feeling for the pen in his pocket as he thought—he would keep a count of every one. He stepped to the edge of the tie-up to meet the low cruiser as its engine cut and the boat glided silently toward the bump. When he reached out he saw that the man holding the rope at the bow was Paleo, the earnest man, Antrina's brother. He had been the last person Darby had seen before he had left his home nearly one month ago. Paleo had equipped Darby with the shoulder bag filled with extra shirts sewn by Antrina. He had left Darby with sandwiches meant to tide him through the long crossing. Paleo had made the event a family parting, flushing with unexpected affection, repeating with undue precision the instructions that Darby would need to follow. Here, now, twenty-eight days afterward, Darby grinned at the sight of him.

"I thought for sure we would find you right around here," Paleo said from the bow. "We made many stops on the way downstream from here yesterday. We didn't find you at any of those but some of them knew about you working up here so I figured today would be the day that we would find you. I'm very glad that we finally did. We came a long way. And this isn't the safest time to be traveling. Especially not for us. I'm a soldier now. A lieutenant. Finally I figured it was time to come back from America to help with the fighting. Before I left for here Antrina told me when I found you I had to say her hello for her. And to tell you to be careful and not to get hurt. She said when she comes here herself she will see you and in the meantime you're supposed to be very careful and not to get hurt."

Paleo and the pilot stepped from the wave cutter to the wharf. Paleo explained, "this is my captain. This is Captain Actus." The small man clicked himself upright in a form of salute. He snapped out his arm to shake hands with Darby.

"I am very glad that we found you too," Actus said. "The lieutenant has said many good things about you to me."

"I told him you are just right for our army," said Paleo. "That is why we came up this river here to look for you. We are on a recruiting mission. Captain Actus comes out sometimes to sign up more soldiers. Don't be worried about how we came dressed. We can't dress in our uniforms of course, because then we would be caught and found out for sure. But we came out to sign up more soldiers and I suggested to Captain Actus that we should come up this way here because this is where you were heading when I left you in America the last time."

"I am prepared to offer to make you an officer," said Captain Actus. "Only an Entry Lieutenant, of course. But the way things are going, you should have plenty of chances to move up."

"But can we talk to you about all of this inside?" asked Paleo. "It's not too safe for us to stay out here for too long. Not on a day like today with their eye in the sky and everything. Can we go inside this building right here?"

Darby led the two men inside the low shed. He brought

them to the closed-in corner, where he switched on the rattling air conditioner.

"Are all of those boxes out there cigarettes?" quizzed Paleo.

"Yee," said Darby. "Dey aller de ciggies."

Paleo and the captain exchanged collusive glances. Darby pulled open a drawer in the metal cabinet that stood askew to the wall. He dipped in both hands to lift out a scoop of cellowrapped ciggie packs. He spilled them onto the desk and then he fished in another drawer for a handful of match books which he also dropped onto the desk. Captain Actus performed a subtle half-bow in expression of gratitude. He took a pack from the desktop and peeled open its top.

"So this must be where you work?" said Paleo.

"Ei workie ewside," said Darby. "Ei load de boasts ewside. De boss ee workie enside in disses room."

"Where is this boss right now?" Paleo asked him.

"Doan know."

"Is he usually in here?"

"Allerways here."

"A-ha," said Paleo. "Then I think I can tell you where he is. Well, I can't tell you exactly where he is right at this moment. But I can tell you for sure why he is not here and I can tell you for sure that you will not see him for the whole rest of today. We run into this same thing every place we go. We ran into it all the places yesterday. When we come out recruiting the word travels out ahead of us. Men find out we'll be here and they run and hide for the day so they don't have to see us. We ran into it all over the places we stopped at yesterday. Not every man, of course, but some men run and hide for the day. When we get to a place people say that if we want good soldiers then we should go to see this guy or we should go to see that guy. But when we try to find those guys they're not around and nobody can tell us where to find them. They're not where anybody expects them to be because they're not in the places where you can usually find them because they're hiding. They like to think they're too important to sign up so they go away and hide for the whole day. They like to think the only reason they're not already in the army is because they're doing something too important that has to get done and therefore they can't leave it. That's what they say but really I think they're afraid we just aren't going to ask them so they hide away to get out of the embarrassment of not being asked to sign up. We don't want men like them. We wouldn't even ask them to join and that's why they stay away: to get out of the embarrassment. They hide for the day so they can feel like it's them who decided. They save face to themselves, so they can say that they'd be in the army if only they weren't so valuable here. But even if they were here right now in this room, we wouldn't ask them. We'd let them stay. The army doesn't want them. It doesn't want any men like your boss and I bet you won't see him back here for the whole day today because he doesn't want me to tell him that we don't want him. That's why he's not here today when any other day he would be sitting right here where we're sitting right now. So I don't mind it at all when I'm taking his cigarettes," said Paleo, who snatched a pack for himself from the desktop.

"But I'm very glad you're here," he said, "because we want you to join up with the army. We're here to ask you to, I mean. To join up with the Borto army. It's better than staying here. Look at it: there's nothing for you to stay here for. What did you say you're doing here? You're loading up the boats for the smugglers? That's okay when it's the only thing there is for you to do. But in the army you can do a lot more. Captain Actus can make you an Entry Lieutenant right away and after that, who knows? I told him already that you're a real good guy and you're a real good leader and you're just the kind of guy we need to recruit. So here we are. It's okay for you to stay here if you want but this is not the place for you. In the army you'll be doing something that's very important.

"I don't mean because we're fighting against Americans. I know that part might seem hard for you. But you can't really think of it like that. We're not really fighting against them. We're Americans ourselves. That's how we think of ourselves. That's why we come and go so easy between the two places. That's why my sister Antrina can live there for so long and I can go there to work. We're all Americans and there's even some Americans in the Borto army and there's some Bortos in the American army. It's all the fussy rules that started this. That's what we're fighting against. The fussy rules. They tell us where we should live and what kind of cars to drive, how we should use our land and then they take it away in taxes and all that stuff. Everybody just had enough of that.

"They had enough of Bortus, too. Bortus was just no good but he had all the power because he could get so much money and so much other things from the America government as long as he made sure all the fussy rules got followed."

"Of course, Bortus won't be bothering us anymore," Captain Actus contributed. "The problem now is getting rid of the American army that we made very angry when we were getting rid of Bortus."

"That's right," said Paleo. "And it's a very good army. I want you to know that. So I can't say this isn't very dangerous. But we're not doing so bad with the fighting. I know you heard about Ridish and Convey. But those weren't complete losses. I was at Convey. That happened right after I came back here to fight. And look: I'm still around. Captain Actus too. And of course you heard about our big victory at Belnish. That's where we showed everybody we mean business. That's where General Flavin crossed the River Narfink when the storm was so bad that two other commanders didn't even try to get their men across. They were going to cross at some other places but the storm got worse so they didn't even try to make it across. Only General Flavin did. And then he captured the whole town of Belnish and all of the soldiers there. It was a great victory."

"So far we've been very lucky upstairs," added Captain Actus. "So far they have done very little damage with their sky power."

"That's right. The only thing they attack from the sky is Bortus's buildings," Paleo explained. "All of his ministries of this and his ministries of that. Who knows why. All of those places are deserted now. All his workers left those places when Bortus ran off himself and we don't care about any of those places. They're Bortus's. We don't care if anybody blows them up. Maybe we'd blow them up ourselves if the American pilots didn't do it for us already."

"But still," said Actus, "if they came after some of our encampments from the sky . . .."

"That's right," followed Paleo. "So I don't want to make it sound like it's not real dangerous. And if my sister Antrina knew what I was doing right now she would be real mad at me, same as she was real mad when I came here myself to fight. I came here just eleven days ago. No, wait, it was twelve. I came here myself just twelve days ago. But I think you'll be doing something real good if you come to join up with us. You can make a contribution to something that's real important. Why would you stay here instead? There's no reason why you would stay here instead."

"Ye helpie mim."

"Yes," said Paleo. "That's right. I explained already to Captain Actus how you are a good friend to us with my sister Antrina and how when you were in that little trouble we helped you out of it by helping you to come here."

"Dey chet-em mim."

"They cheat you?" asked Paleo. "Who cheats you?"

"De boss-ee chet-em mim wid de pidem mim."

"I don't think you're with real good people here," said Paleo.

"Ye mekka mim lit-man?"

"Yes," replied Captain Actus. "I am prepared to make you an Entry Lieutenant. Of course, that is only a junior grade, but there is plenty of room to move up because we have great need for good officers. Your friend Lieutenant Paleo here started as only an Entry Lieutenant, and now he has already advanced a grade. That was after Convey, of course, where our needs increased a great deal. But you see that there's room. Now, where you end up—what job, what unit, and ultimately what rank—will depend upon what you can do. That will just have to be seen. But this is a very good start."

After Darby agreed to join them, Actus and Paleo arranged to stop for him early the next morning, as they motored back downstream.

"I don't think we should stay in this town any longer today," said Paleo. "We already stayed long enough. And by getting you to sign up with us I think we already did enough here. Now we can head up the river some more to the bigger towns up there. We can finish our day up there. We have better chances up there anyway. We need some good grunts. We'll send them along and then we'll tie up and sleep and early in the morning when we're coming back we can stop here for you to get in."

"That leaves only the matter of the cigarettes," said Actus.

"The cigarettes?" wondered Paleo.

"Yes, the cigarettes: should we take some crates now, or wait till we come back tomorrow?"

"Are you in charge of all of these?" Paleo asked Darby.

Darby shrugged. "Ei owny lewdee-um," he answered.

"Do you think we can take some?"

"Ye tekke dem aller."

"Well," smiled Paleo, "we hardly have room for all of them. But if we can put some in the boat to take back, that will be very good. That will be very appreciated."

"Ei lewdee-um fer ye," Darby affirmed.

"But we are coming back tomorrow, don't forget," said Captain Actus. "That still leaves us the question, should we take some crates now, or wait till tomorrow?"

Paleo asked: "the man who is in charge here, the man who went hiding today, do you think he will be back here tomorrow?"

Darby shrugged. "Mebbee."

"Then I say probably we should load it right now," said Paleo. "Now we have the opportunity for sure. We should not let it pass. Who can say what the situation might be for us when we come back here in the morning. Who can say how much time we might have when we stop then. It will be better for us to do it right now when we know we can do it for certain. But you don't have to load it up for us," he said to Darby. "I can carry boxes too, you know."

"Nee, nee," said Darby. "Ei lewdee."

"I think Lieutenant Darby is right," Captain Actus broke in. "Let's not forget that the eye in the sky might be watching. I am sure they've been watching Lieutenant Darby load boats for a long time already. If he loads our boat now everything looks the same to them. We want everything to look the same. We don't want any suspicions. I don't think they care about smuggling. I think they like the smuggling as much as we like the smuggling. But I don't think they will feel the same way about our recruiting."

Darby carried the boxes three at a time. He snaked his head around the side of each stack to watch his footing while he walked. He fit fourteen crates below the deck of the inadequate cruiser. At one point Paleo chided him, saying, "make sure you leave enough room for the people. We have to sleep down there tonight. And after we pick you up here tomorrow you will want some room to sit yourself."

As Darby pushed the boat away from the wharf Paleo called to him from the bow: "very good, then, Gadubby. Don't wave goodbye to us unless you always wave goodbye to all the boats you load. We want no suspicions. You will have to be ready for us early in the morning tomorrow. We think we will come here the same time that we came here today. We don't know that for sure, because it depends on a lot of different things. But that's what we plan to try to do so you must make sure you're ready to come with us early."

Darby just nodded to signify that he understood. He would be ready. He turned back to the shed to face his last day in the river town. He would load all the boats even if the wareman stayed away all the day, as Paleo predicted he would. Darby would accept the payments from the pilots himself, he figured.

At the end of the day he would leave the haul in a drawer in the desk in the nook—after he took out his daily due and after he counted out one extra dollar for every crate that he hefted, just as the smeared and sooty woman had told him to do.

The woman. On some afternoons she bathed. On some evenings when Darby returned from the wharf she wore fresh clothes and he discerned the faint fragrance of soap when he laid his nightly room payment into her palm. Would she wash today, Darby wondered. If not he would send her to the bath. He would not mind the delay, and she would be rewarded when he left her in the morning and gave her every one of the extra dollars that he took for his labors today.

## CHAPTER SIXTEEN

G ab Darby blinked open his eyes in the dull, penetrable gray that preceded the dawn. A shrieking bird pierced the forest canopy over his tent. Blurts and calls from other creatures carried in from the distance. The sounds surrounded him like air. Yet beside him the two other officers slept undisturbed by the racket. Darby listened for their breathing, rhythmic beneath the erratic hollers of the birds. He peered into the dimness. Their supine forms were scarcely discernible inside the inadequate gray. What time did they come in last night, he wondered. He had fallen asleep. He had missed their return after he had laid awake for hours waiting for them. At least it had seemed like hours in the dense, forest blackness that had filled the tent while he waited last night. Captain Andy and Lieutenant Renno had left for their mission unusually late. Therefore their return, whatever the hour, must have been very late as well. Darby felt certain they would sleep even later than usual this morning.

He pushed up carefully from the tent floor. He reached

quietly for the cache of his clothing at the foot of his bag. Quietly, deliberately, he pushed his arms through the sleeves of his camo-top. He buttoned the cuffs around his wrists and he buttoned the shirt-front all the way up. He turned his head side to side to break the tight pinch of the collar around his neck. After he hitched up his trousers Darby carried his boots outside the tent, stepping lightly and staying well clear of the two sleeping men.

He had to peer very hard through the dimness to stay on the trail that led down to the wheelyard. The way wasn't worn very clearly, because only Darby, Andy and Renno ever walked it—and then only once or twice a day. Captain Andy and Lieutenant Renno had set their tent far apart from any others, in a secluded, lush bower where only the wild chatter of the forest or else its blunted silence ever reached. The path led only to the wheelyard, where the three officers worked. Darby walked down there early each morning largely for solitude among the trucks. He liked to arrive before any of the others arrived simply to perform some labors that might count as a contribution, no matter how small. Later, when his tent-mates arrived and when the enlisted men came up from the separate trail that rose along the river bank, their simple presence excluded Darby from the tasks he felt he could perform. The physical chores went to the soldiers. The officers supervised—or else they just loafed, since so many of the day-to-day chores at the yard required no real supervision. The situation left Darby with nothing to do. He idled the time extraneously. Mostly he just listened to the baffling talk, unable to contribute much substance himself. He felt bored. He felt excluded. He felt unnecessary, except at the start of the day, when he walked alone to the abandoned yard, before any of the others arrived to take back their legitimate jobs.

Andy and Renno had led the trucks out late yesterday carrying troops to somewhere or other. When he reached the yard alone in the morning Darby found them skewed and jumbled, tossed haphazardly into the spaces that the soldiers had hacked clear for them weeks ago—another sign that the trucks had returned very late in the night. Only their engine-ends hid beneath the metal-mesh canopies that stretched between tree trunks like tents or lean-tos to screen out any snooping space eyes that managed to penetrate the dense, green, growing tangle of limbs and leaves overhead. Darby counted the trucks carefully, plucking a finger to mark each one. Just twelve had returned. One must still be out, he thought. Or maybe it had been damaged or destroyed.

Darby reached behind the seat in a truck cab to pull out the worn, nubbly broom that the soldiers kept stashed there. He climbed into the truck's wide, open back and —working mostly by feel in the inky shadows beneath the Conestoga cover—he started to sweep the front corners of the cargo box. He pushed clods, chunks, splinters and grit into a furrow that he worked toward the open tailgate at the back. When he finished the first truck and prepared to jump down to tackle a second, he saw that the woman, Jean, the clerk from the command tent, had arrived at the clearing at last.

Jean was American, like Darby. She came to the wheelyard very early most mornings for the same reason as Darby—or, if not quite for solitude, she came seeking privacy. She came to escape foul, teeming exposure in the baths and latrines at the crowded main camp. She came in the dimness like Darby, before any others arrived, to shower discretely with the hose that Renno had rigged for hot water by sucking heat from a truck's engine. After she washed and dried and dressed, typically she lingered with Darby. She stayed close beside him as he worked. She spoke quietly. She pattered idly about the mere state of the day. She didn't expect Darby to reply to her. Jean was gentle and undemanding. She asked for nothing from Darby except for some silent composure. Therefore she did not diminish the solitude that Darby enjoyed. In fact, in her way she seemed to complement the placid dawn, perhaps just by witnessing Darby's claim to it.

But this morning Jean did not wash with the hose. On the ground at her feet she rested a duffel, crammed full, stretched taut and bulging. A combat helmet sat heavily on her head. Jean peered down carefully at papers clipped onto her board, more of the orders she seemed always to courie around the camp.

She looked up at Darby and smiled.

"I don't know if you'll have time to broom them all," she said.

She fingered through the papers. She looked up at Darby again.

"I have to make sure I leave the right ones," she explained.

She pulled a sheaf of the pages free from the clipboard and threw them backward over her shoulder with almost a playful air. She goosed her neck around to look at where they landed on the ground just behind her.

"I guess maybe they'll scatter on their own," she said. "It's supposed to look natural anyway. Like they were left behind by accident. If anybody finds them they're supposed to read them and think we have a lot more trucks and vehicles and things than we really have. The whole thing seems kind of silly to me. I mean, they could just count up the tracks and the spaces and stuff to find out exactly how many trucks we have. I guess maybe they figure they'll believe papers before they believe all the other things they see."

Darby nodded. The woman bent her head again to look through the pages that remained on her board. She looked up at him again and smiled uncertainly. She gazed around the motor compound.

"I'm surprised no one else is down here yet," she said. "I didn't want to be the last one, but it looks like we're both way early."

Darby nodded.

"I can help you sweep," she said. "Do you have another broom?"

Together they climbed into a truck box. Starting in front, they pushed the grit into a linear ridge that they walked toward the open tail. Just when they finished a pair of wheelyard workers spilled into the clearing from the trail that led up from the stream. Others straggled up the path. The men gathered into a dissolute knot. They yawned. They shuffled. They dropped large, stuffed gear bags to the ground at their feet. Lieutenant Renno and Captain Andy came in from the other direction. The officers threw down four duffels, each one stuffed and bulging.

"We packed up your stuff for you, Gab," blared Captain Andy. "You were asleep so deep when we got back last night that we didn't want to wake you up just to tell you that we're moving out this morning. We should of figured you'd be down here before the rest of us."

"It's a good thing you don't have too much stuff," joked Lieutenant Renno. "We'd of left it in the woods."

Darby and Jean climbed down from the truck. Darby stepped over to stand next to Andy and Renno. Jean stayed near the truck, suspended between the disinterested soldiers and the three officers who huddled loosely apart from them.

"It looks like we have just enough," said Andy. "I thought we might be short but it looks like we'll have one driver for every truck."

"It's a good thing we had to leave that old barrel wagon behind last night," said Renno.

"Sergeant Linet," called Andy, "is this everyone who's coming?"

"This is all of 'em that was left down there," answered the sergeant.

"And you got everything all packed up?" asked Andy.

Linet closed off a yawn. "Yes, captain," he replied. "This is everything you said for us to take with us."

An explosion burst like a startling rend in the distance. The curse and boom of cannon fire pierced like electrical shock. Clattering small arms erupted. Machine guns stuttered angry stuccatoes. Concussions resonated upward from the ground through the soles of the soldiers' boots. The men standing with Sergeant Linet shuffled anxiously.

"We better get going right away," said Andy more loudly. "Sergeant Linet, get those covers out of the trees and load 'em up right away. You can let the men drive whatever trucks they want. We'll take the ones that are left. We'll have just enough that way: one driver for each truck."

The soldiers spread out right away to collapse the metal-mesh canopies that hung in the trees. Over their heads the roars, raps, booms, cracks, clangs, chonks, thuds and crashes grew like a great, rolling ball that gained speed and momentum.

"Jean, are you coming with us?" Captain Andy called to the woman.

"Yes, sir," she said. "They all moved forward last night. They said I was supposed to ride along with you to wherever we set up again. I'll met up with them there, but I'm supposed to ride along with you."

"Good," beamed Lieutenant Renno, "you can ride in the truck with me."

"Renno, you're gonna be the chaser again," said Andy. "You drive last in the line so if anything goes wrong with any of the other trucks, you can swing up right away and fix it. Don't take too long. If you can't get it moving right away you'll just have to leave it. You won't have much time. Don't leave it unless you have to. We don't want to lose any more trucks if we can help it. But don't get caught fiddling around with anything for too long.

"And Gab," Captain Andy said to Darby, "you're gonna have to drive the fuel truck. You'll come last, at the very end of the line, behind Reno's chaser."

"Bud . . .," Darby began feebly to protest.

"You're the only one left to take it," said Andy. "I can't take it 'cause I gotta lead us all out of here. And you know none of the drivers will take it. They'll leave it for one of us because they never want to drive the fuel truck. Don't worry about it. It's just a superstition. You're the only one left to drive it."

"Bud . . .," began Darby again. A cannon volley tore the ground so violently that the shuddering earth shook the men's knees.

"We don't have time to get into it now," said Andy. "You're the only one left who can drive it."

"Sir," said the woman, Jean, stepping up. "Sir, I think I'd like to drive the fuel truck," she said.

"You?" exclaimed Lieutenant Renno.

"Yes, sir," she said. "I already know how to drive it, but I'm supposed to get more practice. They said I should get more

177

practice and make sure I know how to drive all the trucks because I might need to drive one if we get really short-handed."

"Who told you that," Renno demanded.

"They told me that before they went forward last night, sir."

The rancorous din rolled nearer.

"Just take it," said Andy. "I don't care which one of you drives the damn thing. Trade off it you want. Let's just get out of here. Let's get out of here right away."

Jean climbed into the driver's seat. Darby hefted their duffels into the cab. He wedged them side-by-side on the floor so that he had to raise his knees high to rest his feet on the bags. The pair sat in silence as they watched the eleven trucks file one by one onto the narrow, rutted trail that led out of the clearing. The path was scarcely wider than the trucks themselves. Shaggy green vegetable walls crowded both of its sides. Limbs arching over the top of the roadway formed a dank tunnel.

As Jean at last edged the truck slowly forward to file in as last in the line, she asked Darby, "Why doesn't anybody else want to drive this?"

"Fire," he replied.

"They're afraid of a fire?"

"De fire frommy de missile-hit," he explained. "Dey shewt-is dis truckie de first."

"Oh. They think they'll shoot at the fuel truck before they shoot at any of the others."

"Yee," said Darby.

"I didn't mean to cut you off back there," Jean said. "With Captain Andy, I mean. I didn't mean to cut you off but it just seemed like the best way to handle it. Nobody really said that I needed to learn how to drive this. But I needed an excuse. I thought it would be easier if I told them that because they don't always understand that a lot of people in America don't learn how to drive. I don't think Captain Andy was ever there before. It just seemed like this would be easier than trying to explain to him that you never learned to drive. He wouldn't understand."

Darby nodded.

"And I really didn't want to ride with Lieutenant Renno," she said.

Darby nodded again. Jean struggled to tuck the tanker close behind Renno's chaser in the rear. But the caravan raced out faster than she could follow. The fuel truck was fully loaded. It revved, rumbled, chugged and strained beneath its weight. It bounced and swayed violently on the rutted trail. Jean muscled the wheel as she stayed on the engine to try to catch up.

"Ye drife in Meerka?" Darby asked her.

"Yeah. I drove in America. That's where I learned. Not big trucks like this. I learned to drive trucks in the army. In America I just drove a regular car. I lived out where I had to drive, so I could still get permission and everything."

The trucks ahead of them disappeared around a curve where the closed-in walls made the trail appear as though it simply stopped in a shadow. Jean tried to force the fuel truck faster. She backed off when the wheel nearly jerked from her grip.

"Everyone over here drives," she said. "Even in the urbs. They wouldn't understand that you never learned how. I think they already wonder enough about you. I wonder myself. I mean, you're the Slugger. You're the great Ad Man. Everybody knows that. You would mean a lot to everybody over there. On the American side, I mean. Instead you're over here and all you do is cover it up. I don't get that. Why aren't you over there?"

she asked him.

"Ei missed de ground ball," he said. Then, as if it would make the explanation clearer, he added, "Ei missied et in de Bic Game."

"I know about that," she said. "But I still wonder why you're here."

"Ye Meerkin too," he told her.

"Yeah, I know, and I don't know what I'm doing here myself. It all seemed the same to me after a while. I was married there, you know. Not for too long, but I was. He got killed in a battle. I got blamed for it all. That's when I came over here. Both sides seemed the same, so that didn't matter. And I didn't like getting blamed and everything over there."

"Dey chessied ye way," Darby ventured.

"Yeah, I guess in a way they did. I guess in a way you could say that they chased me away 'cause they made me to blame when I wasn't. A sergeant was really to blame. None of that ever came out but it was really a sergeant that caused it. He just lost all his nerve. We got caught in an ambush. That was a really long time ago. At least it seems like a really long time. I was married then. To the lieutenant in charge of my platoon. Lieutenant Jim Ready. That's why I got blamed for it all, because you're not supposed to be married to someone else who's in the army. I don't even know why I was. Jim just kept asking me and asking me. He wouldn't give up. He was just too tired of just fucking all the time. And he told me he loved me, and, well, how many times in your life are you gonna hear that? So we got married and we kept it a secret except everybody knew about it anyway. It didn't really matter. But then we got ambushed. My husband, Jim, he was up with the first squad and they got pinned down right away. I was back in the second squad and he called back for us to come up on his flank and drive 'em away. I know he did 'cause I heard the call. But the platoon sergeant in charge back there just wouldn't do it. He lost his nerve. He just kept us back there while the first squad was getting all shot up and pretty soon we got pinned down too. Only three of us got out. It was awful. Only three of us got out and I was one and the platoon sergeant was one. When it was all over he told 'em Jim never called up the second squad. Jim did. I know he did 'cause I heard it. But the sergeant said he never did and he said he was married to me and that was all they needed the hear. They blamed me for it. They said Jim didn't call up the squad 'cause he was protecting me so I ended up getting all to blame for everything."

Jean eased the fuel carrier laboriously around the dark curve that had made the vehicles in front of them vanish. Distantly, on the trail ahead of them they saw Lieutenant Renno standing outside of his truck. Another truck was stopped with his. When Renno saw Jean and Darby he waved frantically for them to approach. Jean coaxed the lumbering tanker to move a little faster. When she reached Renno she let off the pedal so that the awkward fueler stopped simply from the rub of its wheels in the road's deep ruts. The clatter of battle roared in through the truck's open windows, discernible again above the low idle of the engine.

Renno ran to Jean's window.

"The stupid bastard ran out," he shouted as he gestured toward the truck stopped in front of his. "Get it filled right away. We gotta get going. Get the hose out. We gotta get out of here fast as we can."

A fresh convulsion of gunfire broke violently to the right of them. Darby and Jean clambered down from the cab. Jean tugged ahead with the hose nozzle while Darby stayed at the fuel truck to work the pump. Near on their right the sprays and pops and short brilliant cackles were answered by nicks and claps that swelled to a steady rumble.

Renno fished out a cigarette from a package he pulled from his breast pocket. "I can't believe this," he vexed. "I can't believe this stupid bastard ran out of fuel right here."

The truck's driver, watching Jean as she worked, shrugged nervously. "The gas gauge is broken," he said. "It's always been broken. I think someone should of fixed it by now. I thought it was full 'cause it was supposed to be filled up last night. Someone forgot this one. It's not my fault. It was supposed to be full."

Renno sucked furiously on his cigarette. "I come up here and the stupid bastard is looking inside the hood as if there's something wrong with the engine."

"It's not my fault," said the driver. "Somebody should of filled it last night."

Fuel spun through the hose. The driver shuffled nervously. Renno sucked his cigarette furiously. A squad of Borto soldiers approached from up the road, creeping toward the fight that closed in behind the trucks. The grim soldiers parted and streamed around the vehicles, pushing anxiously against the vertical mat of vines and scrub and small trees that edged the road, holding their rifles up at the ready, cowing open their eyes. A young lieutenant nodded a hasty greeting to Darby as he passed with the fighters. Darby nodded silently back to him. Fuel spun through the hose. Darby glanced backward down the trail toward the stealing soldiers. They approached the bend where the road disappeared. The soldiers crept slowly toward the curve, spread to each edge of the road, each man crouched, stepping carefully, as if only the sound of a footstep might give him away, even though not a sound could be heard above the racket of gunfire that moved viciously up the road.

"That's enough," said Renno. "Let's go. We don't need to fill it all the way up. Let's go."

Jean yanked the hose from the tank before Darby could kill the pump switch. Viscous fuel spewed on the trail. Darby spun the reel rapidly to take up the hose while Jean raced around to the tanker's cab.

Rifle fire burped and sprayed from the squad that had disappeared around the bend in the road just behind them. Renno scrambled into his truck. It roared. It lurched. It jumped. It swerved around the refueled vehicle and raced forward on the forest trail. In the refueled truck the driver leaned forward as he cranked the engine with grave insistence. It caught. The engine hollered and whined as his foot slammed too hastily on the pedal. The truck leaped forward. It bounced and rocked. Ahead of it Renno's racing truck blanked into the shadows and disappeared. Jean edged the tanker close behind the refueled truck to keep up with it. It raced ahead of them. It looked like it would disappear the same way Renno's truck had just disappeared. Then white plumes coughed from its tail pipe. It slowed. Jean tucked in behind it again. The truck crawled too slowly. Behind them the road broke open with clamor and din. The truck ahead lurched. It rolled. It rocked. It coughed. Jean edged her front bumper behind it to push. It rolled ahead of them slightly as it regained some will. Its tail pipe sputtered rank smoke. It bounded forward again. It raced. It roared. It sighed, and then slowly it rolled to a standstill.

Jean steered carefully off of the trail, wedging beside the stalled truck and scraping the hacked shrubs and the spiky young trees and the clutter of vines that crowded the edge of the road. She stopped when their cabs came abreast.

"I told him there was something wrong," shot the driver through his open window. "I knew the engine was bad."

"Can you start it," shouted Jean.

"It won't do anything."

Rifle fire roared behind them.

"Leave it," she shouted. "Ride with us."

Two Borto soldiers ran past the trucks, retreating up the road.

"Not with you," said the driver. "I'm not riding in that tanker. No way."

He bolted down from his cab and sprinted to catch up with the fleeing soldiers.

"Shit," said Jean. "Get the weapons out of his truck. We don't have any in here."

Darby kicked open his door and climbed across to the abandoned cab. He took two, stubby rifles from the clip rack beneath the dash.

"The ammo box too," Jean yelled to him.

She scarcely waited for him to climb back into the cab before she pushed the tanker onward again, rocking it around the dead truck and dropping its wheels into the ruts that it could ride almost like rails. Darby wedged the metal box of bullets between his feet that sat high on the duffels. He straddled the rifles across his lap. Jean stayed insistently on the accelerator pedal while the engine roared a protest. The road was too rough. She eased off the pedal. Another group of soldiers overtook the truck, retreating up the road faster than the tanker could motor. Darby leaned out the window watching them scurry. He exchanged another fast nod with the young lieutenant who had led the squad into the fight just a few moments earlier.

"They're right behind us," the officer shouted.

Jean yelled across the cab to Darby: "Load those."

He stared down at the two rifles stuck over his thighs.

"Can you shoot?" she asked him urgently.

Darby stared down. Paleo had showed him how to shoot right after Darby's recruitment. And he had fired at targets with his tent mates Andy and Renno in the wide clearing beside the stream. But that had been play, with the other men loading the rifles and Darby just squeezing off rounds.

"Listen to me," demanded Jean. "Take two clips out of the box and load 'em in there." She pointed quickly at the hole below one rifle's chamber. "Put a clip in each one. They'll snap right in. You'll feel it click in place when you got it right. Then pull back on this knob here and let it spring forward. Then you're loaded. Then all you have to do is switch off the safety right there and you can shoot it."

"Kay," affirmed Darby.

"When you shoot it, just point. Just point at who you want to shoot at. It'll shoot every time you pull the trigger. After you shoot all eighteen, you have to put another clip in. Press here to get the empty one out and then put a full clip in just like you loaded the first one."

Darby nodded. He snapped an ammunition clip into each gun. He wedged one rifle in the gap between their seats, so that Jean could grab it easily. He opened his door and pivoted to jump. He figured that if he ran back to the disabled truck, he could hide beneath it and fire from there, giving the woman more time to retreat up the road.

"What are you doing?" she shouted at him as he leaned to jump. She clawed at his back and caught her hand in his waistband.

"Ei slow em," he said.

"No," Jean insisted. "No. Don't get out. I'm not going to leave you here. I'm not. If you get out then I'm getting out too. I'll stay right here with you. I'm not leaving you here alone. I'm not going to go through all that again."

Darby pushed back into the cab. He snapped his door shut. He laid the rifle across his lap with its muzzle stuck out of the window.

"I'm not leaving you behind just to get myself out," Jean repeated. "I don't care what happens."

She urged the truck forward insistently. Darby stuck his head out the open window and watched the road behind them. All the Borto fighters were ahead of them now. Any soldiers who crept up from their rear would be enemy. But Darby couldn't see far before the trail disintegrated into indiscernible shadows. He figured they would see the truck first, before Darby could spot any of them. He wondered if he would hear the spit and hiss of a shoulder-fire launching. He wondered if he would know, for even an instant, that the missile approached the truck. He wondered if he would discern the concussion and explosion in the eye-blink before it engulfed the whole cab, or if oblivion would catch him too quickly.

"Look," Jean shouted.

Borto soldiers stood on the roadway ahead. A whole platoon of them clung to the edges, crouching tensely near the curtains of trees at both sides, while in the center of the road two officers argued passionately, as though they were not even a part of the larger confrontation. They stopped abruptly and turned to face the truck when they heard its protesting engine. Darby recognized the young lieutenant who had passed him both ways on the trail. As the truck drew near the lieutenant ran up meet it. He shouted through the window to Jean. "Hurry through," he said. "They're setting up mines. They were gonna set them up right away but I told them you were coming. I told them they had to wait. They didn't want to wait but I told 'em they had to. Hurry through. There's more of us around the bend up there. That's where we're making a stand."

As they drove through, Darby met the gaze of the second officer, the one who was setting the mines. He was Paleo. The two men recognized each other at once. Paleo's jaw dropped open in surprise.

"That's Gab Darby," Paleo shouted. He turned to the young lieutenant and shouted more excitedly, "don't you know who that is? That's Gab Darby. What's he doing up there in a truck?"

## CHAPTER SEVENTEEN

President Jeannie Welk-Emerson-Landose listened incredulously to the battle account.

"But how did they kill so many of our soldiers?" she asked.

"Don't concentrate on the casualties," pleaded the viewed head of General Handscome, speaking from only one corner of the big screen on the President's conference-room wall. President Jeannie had convened General Handscome along with all her top advisers, bringing them together on the screen that was segmented into eight simultaneous view ports, creating a grid of eight animated faces stuck up on the wall. They belonged to Anton Creps, Director of Public Confidence, to Shea Hin, Secretary of Environmental Policy, to First Labor Secretary Sandi Optet, Press Secretary Sheri Rue, Campaign Czar Bren Drink, Defense Aide Fred Antic, and to Diplomat Albert Diplec. The eighth port held the image of General Handscome. The President herself, along with First Adviser Mel Santee, sat alone at the big table, craning upward at the illumined images of the eight simultaneous talkers.

"Don't concentrate on the casualties," said General Hand-scome. "Some casualties are inevitable. They're unavoidable. But those troops did not die in vain. I can assure you of that. Look at our great accomplishment. We routed the Bort army. They had built up a real tough strong-hold in the jungle. That was the one place they thought they could beat us. But we went in and we rooted 'em out. Now we have 'em on the run."

"But we lost so many," said President Jeannie. "How many did we lose?"

"We lost twelve hundred and thirty two," said First Adviser Santee.

"Twelve thirty two!" guffed the President.

"And I'll bet there'll be more," said Santee, "'cause ya still got all those wounded ones. I'll bet some of those wounded ones are pretty bad. I'll bet some of 'em die and add to the count."

"Well, sure . . .," started the general.

"How did we lose so many?" demanded President Jeannie.

"It's like I said just a minute ago," answered General Hand-scome. "It was their tricks."

"But what *kind* of tricks?"

"Their tricks. Like all those logs they burned. When we first saw those images we had no way of knowing they were burning logs. I saw them myself. I thought for sure they were soldiers. Our IR-eye showed 'em clear as can be. They did all the right movements, too. We saw the trucks come up and we watched 'em go back that same night. We saw all the troops they left behind. Hundreds of 'em, waiting there on the ground in an ambush. But it was just those damn logs. They laid 'em on the ground like exes and they set them on fire so that when they smoldered and burned they looked like they were men laying down. You have to remember that they were under all those trees. Our IR-eye doesn't do as well when it has to look through so many trees. But we thought we had 'em plain as can be. But like I just said a second ago, after our big bombardment, after we sent in our troops to clean up, we found out it was a trick. It was only them logs and there weren't any Borto troops any place in sight. Of course, by then we were all out of position, so when they attacked it was a complete surprise."

"How could burning some wood make it a complete surprise?" asked the President. "And even if it was, how could you ever lose twelve-thirty-two?"

"They were good fighters," the general replied.

"I thought we were supposed to be the good fighters."

"Twelve-thirty-two is way too many," said Santee. "We're never gonna be able to explain twelve-thirty-two. Anton," he asked to the image of Anton Creps, director of public confidence, "can you think of any ways we can explain the twelve-thirty-two?"

"Not really," said Creps. "The polls have stayed very consistent all along: the voters will accept no casualties."

"But we routed 'em," interrupted General Handscome.

"So we routed 'em," said Creps. "That's great. Victory is great. Everyone's for victory. But you aren't supposed to lose any troops. You lost twelve-thirty-two. That's the problem. The voters are going to be really upset."

"That's the last thing we need now," said Santee. "Not with the election so soon. The Antis have already gained too much on us. Anton, what's the latest numbers on how much they've gained?"

"The latest poll?" asked Creps, the public confidence man. "It's pretty much the same as its been. I mean, we're the same place we were when we polled on last Tuesday. We're ahead still, but not by much. And that was before this news gets out. I mean, nobody out there knows about all these losses yet. How many were there?"

"Twelve-thirty-two," said President Jeannie.

"Nobody knows about this twelve-thirty-two yet," said Creps. "Wait till word gets out about that. That's not going to help us. That's not going to help us at all."

"Could it put us behind?" Santee asked him.

"It might. I think it probably will."

"I don't see how this could happen," complained President Jeannie. "I don't see how you could lose so many troops in just one battle."

"It's not *that* many," ventured General Handscome.

President Jeannie glared sharply at his image in the corner of the wall.

"I mean, compared to other wars it's not that many," he said. "Geez, look at all the wars they did in the last century. Look at World War Two, for Christ's sake. In that one war alone we lost more than four-hundred-thousand troops. Four-hundred-thousand! And that was just one war."

"Yeah, but remember your history," Santee said. "They had Hitler to be up against. Hitler was the best bad guy of all times. Everybody hated Hitler. All we got now is Vestin. Sure, everybody hates Vestin. We've done all right with Vestin." Santee glanced sidelong across the table at the President to watch her reaction, wary of disapproval. "But he's not like Hitler was. Hitler was worth four-hundred-thousand. But this time it's different. Nobody hates Vestin twelve-thirty-two worth."

"Everything was easier then," said Shea Hin, Secretary of Environmental Policy, a grave visage speaking near the center of the wall. "The whole war was easier. Back then the services didn't need to file EI Statements. It was just win at all costs, and nobody had any idea how much damage they were doing. They just didn't care."

"Sure," said Santee, "but sometimes ya gotta look at the big picture. You know what I mean? Sometimes ya gotta look at, you know, at the greater good. Like now. Now ya gotta look at the fact that, who's better for the environment? Is it us, or is it the Antis? It's us, of course. So if the Antis take over, I mean, if they win this election, then overall things are gonna get a lot worse for the environment. Right? You see what I mean now? So this time maybe doing some damage down in the rainforest way down in Bortinca is okay. Maybe it's okay as long as it lets us stay in power here. You see what I mean? Maybe right now the best thing we can do is just bomb 'em. Bomb 'em till there's nothing left of 'em. Forget about the damage it'll do to the environment. At least we won't lose any casualties that way. That's what we have to think about now. We have to think about winning this thing once and for all without losing any more casualties. We have to think about winning this thing for the good of the environment. The best way to do that is to bomb 'em. And I mean right now. We don't have any time left. What's the status of our impact statement?"

"It's under review," Hin answered.

"Still?" said Santee. "Can't you speed it up any?"

"Oh, sure," answered the secretary. "I can speed it up and get it done for you today. But you know they'll only challenge it in court. They'll get some judge to put a stay on it and that'll tie it up even longer. At least this way, with a long review, we can argue that we gave it a good going over."

"What are we supposed to do till that happens?" asked

President Jeannie.

"We can't bomb anything outside of their cities," said Hin.

"We can't really do anything," offered the image of First Labor Secretary Sandi Optet. "I mean, whatever we do, we got to stop fighting 'em on the ground. That's for sure. I mean, we just can't lose any more. We just can't risk it. We've already lost too many. Way too many."

"But we can't just let 'em win," said Press Secretary Sheri Rue.

"They didn't win," said General Handscome. "We routed 'em."

"I get asked that every day," said Press Secretary Rue. "'What are we doing to win the war?' Let's not forget that we're supposed to be winning this thing."

"We *are* winning," said the general.

"She's right about that," said Santee. "We can't just run away from them. That wouldn't look any good, either. That's why we gotta bomb 'em. We gotta bomb 'em right away."

"But I just told you that the environmental impact statement is still under review," said Shea Hin.

"Then we can just announce that we plan to bomb 'em," Santee ventured. "Then at least it will look like we're ready to do something."

"But it'll look terrible if you announce it in advance," countered Hin. "It'll look like it was fixed all along. Then they'll get the courts to stop it for sure."

"Then the only thing left to do is just stall," said Santee. "The only thing left to do is just sit there. Well, maybe not sit there. We can move around some. But if we can't bomb 'em, we sure can't fight any more battles. We can't risk losing another guy. Not now. Not until after the election."

"Can we do that?" asked the President.

"Why not?" Santee shrugged.

"What if they attack us?"

"General Handscome says they're on the run."

"But they attacked us before."

"Yeah," agreed Labor Secretary Optet. "They attacked us at the Narfink and they pushed us back. They certainly caused some casualties then."

"That was in the beginning," offered the general. "We weren't ready for that. They won't be able to do anything like that ever again."

"But even if they don't push us back," said Optet, "they could still make some casualties. We can't lose any more casualties."

"I wish I knew the latest numbers," said Santee. "Anton," he shot at Creps, the director of public confidence, "when are we getting new numbers? When are you gonna get out there and get me some new numbers?"

"We're polling right now, " Creps replied. "We poll all the time. Constantly. You know that. But the numbers we're getting now don't matter anyway, because no one knows about this yet. We have to wait till the news gets out. We have to wait till voters know about these—what is it?—about these twelve-thirty-two casualties. That's the big question. That's what we're waiting to see. But like I already said, we already know how everybody feels about casualties. That hasn't changed at all and we haven't seen any reason why we should expect it to change now."

"Yeah," agreed Sheri Rue, the press secretary. "We need to wait till the news comes out on the vid. Then we'll start to see how bad everyone thinks it is."

"But we can't wait," yipped President Jeannie. "I need to

know what to do."

"Yeah," said Optet, the labor chief. "And we already know it's gonna be bad. It's not like we have to wait to see *exactly* how bad it's gonna we. It's gonna be real bad. We know that for sure."

"And we know what the Antis are gonna say about it, too," said Campaign Czar Bren Drink. "We already know they're gonna attack us on it right away. That's the worst part. They're gonna take those twelve-ninety-eight casualties we got and make 'em part of their campaign."

"It's twelve-thirty-two," said General Handscome.

"What?"

"The casualties. It's twelve-thirty-two. You said twelve-ninety-eight."

"That's still way too many," Drink went on. "The Antis have been preaching let's stop the war. That's the main reason they've gained on us. And every time we get a little set-back, they gain on us some more."

"This is a *big* set-back," said Optet.

"They've been inchin' close to neck-'n-neck," said the pollster Creps. "This time they're probably gonna shoot ahead of us."

"What'll we do then," lamented the President.

"We gotta be ready for their next move," said the election czar. "They've been getting closer and closer to saying that if Nishgaugh is elected, he'll end the fighting right away. He'll pull us right out of this thing. We gotta be ready for that. It'll be their most aggressive stand so far, to say that we're actually getting out. They've stopped just short of saying it so far. So far they've just used the war to dig at us. They haven't come out yet and said they'll stop it. They've been watching it the same way we've been watching it. But now, with this latest, with this twelve-ninety-two, they'll be able to say it definitely. That's going to be their next move. They'll be able to say that if you vote for Nishgaugh, he'll pull us out the day that he takes over as President."

"We just can't have any more casualties," said Optet.

"But pulling us out would be losing," protested Defense Aide Fred Antic.

"It won't matter," said Drink. "It won't matter if we lose. No one will care about winning or losing if we have any more casualties. We just can't have any more. That's the way I see it. We can either win —but I mean win big. Not just win another battle, but win the whole war. We can win it big like that so we stop it that way. Before the election. Then we're heroes. Then the war is over and they can't get us on that anymore. But if we don't win it right away, well, I don't know. The last thing we can do is have any more days like yesterday. Even if we win the battle like that, we can't have any more casualties."

"At least they won't attack us," said Santee. "We're safe if we just wait it out. We can make it look like we're getting ready to win. That'll look good. That'll let us say that we can't pull out now, that it would be a mistake for Nishgaugh to pull us out now, 'cause we're on the verge of winning this thing. We can attack the Antis with that."

"But not if we make any more casualties," said Optet. "If we lose any more, then the whole thing's gonna be over one way or another. The Borts will win the war that way, even if they don't actually beat us. 'Cause the Antis will win the election. Nishgaugh will be President and he'll end the war just by pulling us out."

## CHAPTER EIGHTEEN

Gab Darby sat apart from the score of soldiers who had ranged themselves in two loose ranks that straddled the road where it dipped through a low and sheltered hollow. Small trees grew densely on the inclines that banked both sides of the roadway, giving the men good cover. In fact, it was the last of the good cover. Beyond this spot the terrain opened into treeless vales and eskers and bald-sided hills that provided few places to duck and hide. But here the soldiers felt sheltered and safely concealed. Darby stayed separate from them partly from the prerogative of command. Mostly he stayed separate because he did not share their sullen disaffection. Waiting uncertainly, the soldiers cursed and grumbled and chided in low tones. Darby remained silent. He did not mind waiting, and he could find no other reason to complain. He had endured the same jouncing truck ride as the soldiers and the same two-hour march to this bower. He was not unnerved over wondering what would come next. He settled himself comfortably onto a grassy, seat-like cut in the road's embankment, well in view of the soldiers, but outside the range of their voices.

He leaned back. He began to wonder if he should close his eyes to try to recapture some of the sleep he had sacrificed during the truck ride last night. Before he could decide he saw Paleo hustling toward him on the road. Jean came beside him. She looked fretful and concerned. As the pair drew closer, a column of soldiers appeared on the road behind them. The soldiers moved less eagerly. When Paleo saw Darby sitting in the recess next to the road he turned around and signaled for the column to stop. Jean stayed beside him and together they scurried up to Darby, who rose and smiled before they reached him.

"I'll keep them back there," Paleo blurted, panting for breath. "Those are the reserves. I'll keep them back there till you move your men up."

Paleo gazed ahead at the two rows of soldiers who stood waiting apart from Darby at the sides of the road. The men looked back at him, attentive, in pique. Each of the twenty clutched at his rifle. One soldier glanced down at his thoughtfully and brushed soil from the breech.

Paleo shouted to the sergeant, "did the men eat their rations?" He did not wait for an answer because he could see poly wrappers and shreds of refuse strewn on the road between the two columns of troops.

"You're moving them up," he said to Darby. "This is very important. Let me explain it as fast as I can. It looks like they're setting up defensive positions. They're getting ready to hunker down and it looks like maybe stay there a while. We scouted it out and that's what it looks like. General Flavin wants to attack right away. Before they're set up. While we can still get in. That's why you have to move up right away. They're moving now too and we need to get to the better terrain before they do. The general spelled it all out. This movement here is the most important one. The one you're going to do right now. There's a long hill off to the north. You can call it a ridge in fact, 'cause it stretches out for a pretty long ways. It's only about a half mile up the road from here. Off on the left side. You can almost see it when you get around that bend right there, right where the road starts to climb out of these trees. Start looking for it right away. It's just a long, bare hill that runs kind of parallel with the road. But it's off a little ways. It's not right next to the road."

Darby nodded that he understood.

"If we can get to that ridge, then we'll have a command over all the open terrain on the other side of it. That's where General Flavin wants to push his assault through. On the other side of the ridge. It's like a big, wide avenue over there and he can push all the troops through and hit them before they're dug in and set up and fortified and everything. But only if we have the ridge. If they get it, it would be slaughter to move through the land down below it. That's the problem. We scouted it out and it looks like they're going to set up positions on the ridge. They might be there already. We don't know. The only way to find out is for you to get your guys up there."

Darby nodded. Jean, standing close off Paleo's shoulder, shifted anxiously.

"When you get out of this thicket the road will start to climb," said Paleo. "Follow it for a little ways till where you come to an incline running up kind of steeply on your left. That's a steep little hill that comes just before the big ridge that you have to take. When you come to that first little hill get your guys off the road and get them up over the top of it. You'll be concealed till you get over top of it. After that the whole long ridge will be wide open in front of you. Anyone up there already will have a clear shot at you once you get over that first, steep little hill, so get your guys spread out ahead of time. Get them spread out while you're on the road still and then get over top of that first little hill. On the other side of it the ground dips down and then after that you start right away up the main ridge. You gotta get up there fast. You gotta get up there right away. You gotta beat 'em there. 'Cause if they get there first, well, then you're stuck. If they get up to the ridge before you do, then you'll have to make the toughest assault I've ever seen."

Darby looked past Paleo to Jean.

"If you get there first, if they're not already up at the top waiting for you, go all the way up and then drop down the far side just enough to get your men concealed. Then stay there. You've got to hold it. Hold the top at all costs. After you get over the top I'll bring up this second line so we can secure it. We're only about a half mile away. We won't take long to get there."

Jean returned Darby's look anxiously.

"You have to go right away," said Paleo. "You have to run. You need to get to the top. You need to get there before they do. It might already be too late."

Darby smiled at the woman.

Jean's throat caught. She wanted to scream *don't go* but of course she could not. She wanted at least to say *be careful*, but even those words did not fit alongside the urgent battle instructions. They did not fit with the dark, grim uniforms, the steel-shanked rifles, the brows beneath iron helmets. She could not say them in sight of the somberly waiting soldiers.

Darby turned away from Jean and Paleo and gazed with satisfaction at the twenty fighters who waited for him in two loose ranks along the low margins of the road. Poly wrappers spotted the gaps among them. The soldiers watched back at Darby, anxious, inquisitive.

"They're very good soldiers," Paleo said to Darby's back. "They'll do everything you expect them to do, as long as you're worthy of them. That's the thing: you have to be worthy. They're very good soldiers on the other side, too. Just as good as these. It gets down to which side has the best leader. If you lead them well you will win. Make sure of that. Make sure you lead them well."

Darby faced back round to Paleo and Jean. He smiled. He unfastened the buttons on the shirt cuffs around his wrists. He loosened the buttons that closed the shirt at his chest. He shrugged off the blouse and then he peeled away his drab green tee-shirt, pulling it over his head. He dug into his hip pocket for a small, plastic bottle of bug repellant. Darby squeezed a small pool of the unctious goo into his palm. He spread the oil with deliberate care around his neck and atop his shoulders. He rubbed it over his bulging pectorals. He smeared it down his stomach. Lifting first one arm, then the other, he covered both flanks. Lastly he glistened his arms, coating them entirely.

Darby passed the vial to Jean. He uttered, "cuffer mim im de back," as he turned so that she faced the big *Corolla* that adorned him. She reached over the lettering to start at his shoulders. She kneaded the oil into his illustrated skin. She stayed silent through the ritual. She strained to convey with her hands as she rubbed him some tender sensation. She impressed —or tried to impress—a relation he might discern through ambiguous touch. She let her fingers linger gently in one small, round spot, smoothing his flesh in penetrating arcs that she imagined might transmit her vital energy into him, in order to commingle there. She knew that she could not stay too long, because the same constraining circumstances that stopped her from speaking must also curtail too much touch. She finished with a slow run side-to-side and down across his lower back. She removed her hands with wistful hesitation. Darby glistened entirely.

He spun back round to face her. Smiling, he held out his hand to take the small vial. Jean folded it into her palm.

"I'll keep it for you," she said, getting out those words alone.

Darby smiled at her more broadly. His skin ads glinted like armor: *Pepsi Coke* in bright red and blue all across his broad chest, *Shop Luxury* scrolling down his right arm, *K-Wal Stores* down the left. Darby took up his rifle. He stepped out to the center of the road to show himself to the waiting soldiers. He raised the rifle aloft, holding it with one hand coiled around its icy black muzzle. He poked it high into the air like a beacon. He stretched his other arm upward, holding it parallel and pointing it straight up to the sky. He turned a slow pirouette, before he broke into a trot toward the gazing soldiers.

Paleo ran after him, churning his legs awkwardly until he caught up with Darby.

"Stay low till you get over that first little hill," he shouted to Darby as the two men ran apace. "You'll be well covered till you get to the top of that first hill. Once you get over it, it'll be wide open all the way to the top of the ridge. There'll be hell to pay unless you get there right away. Unless you get there before they do."

Darby turned his head to Paleo and smiled. Paleo stopped and watched as Darby kept on at a steady canter. As Darby ran between the soldiers they closed in behind him and followed, their strapped-on sacks and pouches clattering in dull unison. Jean ran closer, stopping at the spot where Paleo still stood. Silently, shoulder to shoulder, they watched the stalwart column push away from them. They watched Darby and his soldiers disappear around the bend where the rising road carried them out of the safe cover of trees. They watched the blank roadway, staring silently at the spot where the group had disappeared. They waited. They listened. They scarcely breathed for fear that the sound might obscure some faint hint of Darby's progress. Six minutes passed. A breeze gently brushed the leaves above them. Seven minutes. Paleo's foot scuffed when he shifted his weight. Eight minutes. A wrapper from the soldiers' rations turned over and settled. Nine minutes. A burst of small-arms fire rent the stillness. Jean winced.

"Is that our guys?" she gasped urgently. "Did they make it? Is that our guys firing on the back of the hill?"

"I don't think so," said Paleo. "It can't be. God damn it. It can't be. It sounds too close. It's coming too soon. They must be too late. They must of got beat to the top."

Jean bent into a dash toward the din of the desperate assault. Paleo shouted after her: "Jean," he called urgently, "Jean. Don't go. It's too soon. Don't go yet. Jean. Wait till I move the reserves. We'll go up then. Jean. Wait here. Let them set up a line. I'll bring the reserves after they set up a line. We'll go up then. Jean. Jean!"

She ran more furiously. She flailed. She coursed. She flung herself blindly around the concealing bend. Only the handgun strapped to her waist encumbered her. She charged into the steep and open terrain. The gunfire ahead of her intensified. Bursts, cackles, rasps and drums. Spits and coughs and rattles. She raced toward it. Riffs merged violently. Shots rang together in a trill of unbroken clatter. Sprinting faster toward the clamor, she saw the small hill that Paleo had described, the sharp upward cant of the embankment on the road's left side. She cut perpendicularly up the bank. She stumbled against the restraining slope of the ground. Cresting the top of the swell she stared upward at the disputed hill that now loomed board and high above her. At first glance it looked calm. She saw no appearance of battle. She dashed down into the low hollow that footed the ridge. She crossed its span in bounds. The raps of gunfire subsided. One sharp crack. A cackle. A rip. A thud that sounded from the ground right beside her. She kept on. The gunfire stopped entirely. In the interval Jean scanned the hillside more closely, charging still. At last she discerned the distributed forms of the men in Darby's assault line. The soldiers pressed flat against the hillside. They lay on the ground in a jagged diagonal that raked upward toward the peak. As she ran still Jean scanned the slope far off to the left of the line. A second group lay pressed on the upslope there, in another diagonal jag that skewed upward toward the peak so that the two, sparse lines of cowering men formed a chevron, or maybe an arrow, that pointed toward the ridge top. She looked at the apex, where she knew she would see Gab Darby. He lay there, flat in the grass, as though he was the arrow's tip.

Jean cut toward the spot where he lay. She pushed harder with her thighs against the inhibiting slope. The aspect of his body was all wrong. He sprawled in a slant on the hillside. His arms spewed too carelessly. Jean reached him, but through the patterning of his skin ads she could not see any wounds. A coating of dust matted their colors as it clung to the oil they had spread just before the assault. She knelt beside him. *Pepsi Coke. K-Wall Stores.* Darby did not move.

The gunfire resumed abruptly. A new wave of attackers spilled over the crest of the ridge. Jean looked up into the blitz. Fleet forms rose out of the line of sky above her and descended with unreasonable fury. They fired as they ran. Bullets hissed, whizzed and seethed. They came as a wind, a wave, an onslaught of inexorable force flung into her face. It would topple her if she knelt. On her sides she saw the shapes of Darby's men. They pressed like scattered dots against the hillside. The wind would topple them too. They wavered. They watched her. More likely they watched Darby. They wavered more. The wind might lift them. It might tear them loose and fling them down the inertial slope. The men watched Darby. Kneeling beside him, Jean leaned perilously forward, pushing against the relentless wind to grasp the rifle that had fallen on the slope just above him. Straining to stay boldly upright against the gale, she backed the rifle into her shoulder and fired. She fired again. She steadied from the recoil. She pointed her eye along the barrel-sight. She spotted attackers individually, as though she peered through a pipe. A sudden, dark-clad form popped up against the sky. She fixed on it and fired. The man fell. She saw another bolt upward from a gray, concealing stone. She fired. He fell.

Supporting fire began from the men arrayed at her flanks. She sensed it as a wind, this one blowing upward and opposing the descending fury. The two forces seemed to meet at a center line above her. One checked the other and as the two winds contended the downward assault seemed to stammer. The descending soldiers stopped. They crouched. They wavered. Jean cracked off more shots. She reached into the pouch on Darby's belt to pull out another clip of ammunition. Reloaded, she sighted with deliberate care along the coal-black barrel.

Through the fray she perceived a person beside her: Paleo.

He knelt low like her, clinging near to fallen Darby.

"Is he dead?" Paleo asked.

Jean did not answer. If she spoke a word she would start to cry, and if she cried she could never sight the rifle so accurately. She kept her cheek pressed against the gun stock, aiming resolutely against the forms she saw waver and drop on the grass slope above her. Paleo could see the answer clearly enough anyway.

With Paleo's riflemen aiding the soldiers that Darby had first led up the slope, the wind seemed swiftly the change. The descending gust curled upward. The opponents who had stormed brutally over the ridge began creeping back.

"Take your men up now," Jean said to Paleo between rifle shots. "If you charge up right now you can drive them off and take the ridge."

Paleo looked up at the contended summit.

"Will you stay with him?" he asked her.

"I'll stay right here with him."

He raised himself tentatively, surveying the slope more carefully.

"We'll keep up a covering fire," Jean said. "If you go right away you can make it."

Paleo signaled to the soldiers who had followed him up the hill. They crept forward in a line, dispersed, ascending, each man standing warily at half-height. Jean aimed carefully among them. Opposing soldiers bolted upright and broke for the ridge line in the face of Paleo's advance. Jean fired at a man who stood up suddenly from a slit or a dip that had kept him concealed. He fell. Another groped hastily for the ridge line above him. She sighted. She fired. He ran. He leaped and disappeared over the line at the crest. She scanned for another. Paleo's men abruptly reached the top. Jean pulled back her rifle. She could no longer distinguish targets. She saw just Paleo's men at the top of the ridge. Quickly they disappeared as well, as they clambered over the top to claim the advantage by firing against the downslope.

The cracks, whips, crackles, bangs and whirs that had engulfed her so savagely immediately subsided. The wind stopped. The air grew still. The rifle shots masked by the ridgetop sounded muffled and distant. The place became instantly peaceful.

Kneeling still, Jean looked down at Darby. She reached and strained to place his body in a posture it might find more comfortable. But when she moved him she saw how the grass beneath him was sponged with blood. She pushed him back over the spot to conceal it.

She sat on the ground beside him. She didn't know what she would do. She realized that the men under Darby's command were ranged on the hillside still, strung out in their chevron, watching her.

"He's dead," she shouted. "You don't have to stay here now. Go over the top with Captain Paleo and help him to hold the hill."

She waited silently while the soldiers rose and crept and at last dropped away from her over the summit. When she was the last living person at the bier of Gab Darby, she folded her face into her open hands, and wept.

## GLOSSARY

**allerways** always
**bewt** about
**bic** big
**blasph** curse, darn
**boron** native of Bortinca
**bud** but
**cewp'rate** cooperate
**commies** commercials
**cuffer** cover
**de** the
**dee** do you
**dere** there
**dey** they
**diddy-less** ridiculous
**doan** don't, do not
**ef, effa** if
**efta** after
**Ei** (pronouced *ee*, as *bee*) I

**en-bod** anybody
**en-thin** anything
**er** or
**es** this
**eshly** especially
**espessy** special
**essy** easy
**et** it
**ev** ever
**evna** even
**fer** for
**Gadubby** Gab Darby
**gew** go
**gewin** (also **gwin**) going
**gin** again
**gosta** got to, have to
**gunter** going to
**gwinteh** going to

**hefta** (also **heffta**) have to
**homminy** home
**kay** okay
**kep** keep
**kin** can
**leef** leave
**lek** like
**livvy** live
**luf** love
**mebbee** maybe
**mee** may
**mehr** more
**mek** make
**mim** me
**moor** more
**nee** no
**neh** no; none
**neh-bod** nobody
**ne-mehr** no more
**nevne** never
**nith** neither
**noan** no one
**no-ne** no; not; had not
**nudth** another
**nuth** nothing
**nutnin** nothing
**quewmer** vacuum cleaner
**scen** seen
**scewel** school

**shewwin** showing
**sid** said
**spict** expect
**sumptin** something
**te** (also **tuh**) to
**te-mor** tomorrow
**thawet** thought
**ti-dee** today
**tuh** (also **te**) to
**tuum** to them
**uff** off
**vid** video image; screen
**waffer** what for
**wanner** want to
**way** away
**whir** where
**whud** what
**wid** with
**woan** won't, will not
**wud** would
**yahr** year
**ye** you
**yee** yes
**yer** your; you are, you're
**yes-tiddy** yesterday
**yewd** you'd, you would
**yit** yet

# ABOUT THE AUTHOR

Jeffrey Zygmont writes stories about free people who possess rebellious impulses. His books tell about independent characters in conflict with collected groups and their constraining beliefs. In addition to Ad Man in the Games of 2046, that theme of defiant independence animates two other current novels: I Am Bill Gates' Dog, and The Dropout.

Jeffrey Zygmont's short fiction has appeared in the anthology The Literature of Work, and in periodicals ranging from New Hampshire Journal to the magazine Twin Cities Business Monthly. His poetry has appeared in the journal Not Just Air. Two of his poems received nominations for the annual Pushcart Prize, a respected literary award. They are Wife Poem XXVII, nominated in 2008, and Menopause, nominated in 2009. Zygmont's novel The Dropout was the July 2002 Featured Selection of the pioneering ebook publisher Online Originals.

As a journalist, Zygmont has published articles in magazines and newspapers including Boston Magazine, Boston Woman, Business Week, CFO Magazine, The Christian Science Monitor,

Cigar Aficionado, Gannett Newspapers, Inc Magazine, The Boston Globe Sunday Magazine, and Robb Report. He was the automobile columnist for Omni Magazine, a technology columnist for PC Computing Magazine, and an editor for High Technology Magazine. His non-fiction books are Microchip; An Idea, Its Genesis and the Revolution It Created, and The VC Way; Investment Secrets from the Wizards of Venture Capital, which was translated into Chinese for sale in that country.